The Primrose Ring

Ruth Sawyer

Alpha Editions

This edition published in 2024

ISBN 9789362091963

Design and Setting By
Alpha Editions
www.alphaedis.com

Email - info@alphaedis.com

As per information held with us this book is in Public Domain.
This book is a reproduction of an important historical work.
Alpha Editions uses the best technology to reproduce historical work
in the same manner it was first published to preserve its original nature.
Any marks or number seen are left intentionally to preserve.

Contents

FOREWORD ....- 1 -

I CONCERNING FANCY AND SAINT MARGARET'S........................- 2 -

II IN WHICH MARGARET MACLEAN REVIEWS A MEMORY....- 10 -

III WARD C...- 16 -

IV CURABLES AND INCURABLES ....- 26 -

V ODDS AND ENDS ....- 35 -

VI THE PRIMROSE RING..- 43 -

VII AND BEYOND ....- 50 -

VIII IN WHICH A PART OF THE BOARD HAS DISTURBING DREAMS...- 61 -

IX THE LOVE-TALKER ....- 70 -

X WHAT HAPPENED AFTERWARD ....- 77 -

FOREWORD

DEAR PEOPLE,—Whoever you are and wherever you may be when you take up this book—I beg of you not to feel disturbed because I have let Fancy and a faery or two slip in between the covers. You will find them quite harmless and friendly—and very eager to become acquainted.

Furthermore, please do not search about for Saint Margaret's; it does not exist. I shamelessly confess to the building of it myself, using my right of authorship to bring a stone from this place, and a cornice from that, to cap the foundation I discovered long ago—when I was a child. In a like manner have I furnished its board of trustees. Do not misjudge them; remember that when one is so careless as to let Fancy and faeries into a book she is forced to let the stepmothers be unkind and the giants cruel.

I should like to remind those who may be forgetting that Tir-na-n'Og is the land of eternal youth and joyousness—the Celtic "Land of Heart's Desire." It is a country which belongs to us all by right of natural heritage; but we turned our backs to it and started journeying from it almost the instant we stepped out of our cradles.

As for the primrose ring—reach across it to Bridget and let her give you back again the heart of a child which you may have lost somewhere along the road of Growing-Old-and-Wise.

R. S.

I
CONCERNING FANCY AND SAINT MARGARET'S

Would it ever have happened at all if Trustee Day had not fallen on the 30th of April—which is May Eve, as everybody knows?

This is something you must ask of those wiser than I, for I am only the story-teller, sitting in the shadow of the market-place, passing on the tale that comes to my ears. But I can remind you that May Eve is one of the most bewitched and bewitching times of the whole year—reason enough to account for any number of strange happenings; and I can point out to your notice that Margaret MacLean, in charge of Ward C at Saint Margaret's, found the flower-seller at the corner of the street that morning with his basket full of primroses. Now primroses are "gentle flowers," as everybody ought to know—which means that the faeries have been using them for thousands of years to work magic; and Margaret MacLean bought the full of her hands that morning.

And this brings us back to Trustee Day at Saint Margaret's—which fell on the 30th of April—and to the beginning of the story.

Saint Margaret's Free Hospital for Children does not belong to the city. It was built by a rich man as a memorial to his son, a little crippled lad who stayed just long enough to leave behind as a legacy for his father a great crying hunger to minister to all little ailing and crippled bodies. There are golden tales concerning those first years of the hospital—tales passed on by word of mouth alone and so old as to have gathered a bit of the misty glow of illusion that hangs over all myths and traditions. They made of Saint Margaret's an arcadian refuge, where the Founder wandered all day and every day like a patron saint. Tradition endowed him with all the attributes of all saints belonging to childhood: the protectiveness of Saint Christopher, the tenderness of Saint Anthony, the loving comradeship of Saint Valentine, and the joyfulness of Saint Nicholas.

But that was more than fifty years ago; and institutions can change marvelously in half a century. Time had buried more than the Founder.

The rich still support Saint Margaret's. Society gives bazars and costumed balls for it annually; great artists give benefit concerts; bankers, corporation presidents, and heiresses send liberal checks once a year—and from this last group are chosen the trustees. They have made of Saint Margaret's the best-appointed hospital in the city. It is supplied with everything money and power can obtain; leading surgeons are listed on its staff; its nurses rank at the head. It has outspanned the greatest dream of the Founder—professionally. And twelve times a year—at the end of every month—the trustees hold their day; which means that all through the late afternoon, until the business meeting at five-thirty, they wander over the building.

Now it is the business of institutional directors to be thorough, and the trustees of Saint Margaret's, previous to the 30th of April, never forgot their business. They looked into corners and behind doors to see what had not been done; they followed the work-trails of every employee—from old Cassie, the scrub-woman, to the Superintendent herself; and if one was a wise employee one blazed conspicuously and often. They gathered in little groups and discussed methods for conservation and greater efficiency, being as up to date in their charities as in everything else. Also, they brought guests and showed them about; for when one was rich and had put one's money into collections of sick and crippled children instead of old ivories and first editions, it did not at all mean that one had not retained the same pride of exhibiting.

There are a few rare natures who make collections for the sheer love of the objects they collect, and if they can be persuaded to show them off at all it is always with so much tenderness and sympathy that even the feelings of a delicately wrought Buddha could not be bruised. But there were none of these natures numbered among the trustees of Saint Margaret's. And because it was purely a matter of charity and pride with them, and because they never had any time left over from being thorough and business-like to spend on the children themselves, they never failed to leave a shaft of gloom behind them on Trustee Day. The contagious ward always escaped by virtue of its own power of self-defense; but the shaft started at the door of the surgical ward and went widening along through the medical and the convalescent until it reached the incurables at an angle of indefinite radiation. There was a reason for this—as Margaret MacLean put it once in paraphrase:

"Children come and children go, but we stay on for ever."

Trustee Day was an abiding memory only with the incurables; which meant that twelve times a year—at the end of every month—Ward C cried itself to sleep.

Spring could not have begun the day better. She is never the spendthrift that summer is, but once in a while she plunges recklessly into her treasure-store and scatters it broadcast. On this last day of April she was prodigal with her sunshine; out countryward she garnished every field and wood and hollow with her best. Everywhere were flowers and pungent herby things in such abundance that even the city folk could sense them afar off.

Little cajoling breezes scuttled around corners and down thoroughfares, blowing good humor in and bad humor out. Birds of passage—song-sparrows, tanagers, bluebirds, and orioles—even a pair of cardinals—stopped wherever they could find a tree or bush from which to pipe a friendly greeting. Yes, spring certainly could not have begun the day better; it was as if everything had said to itself, "We know this is a very special occasion and we must do our share in making it fine."

So well did everything succeed that Margaret MacLean was up and out of Saint Margaret's a full half-hour earlier than usual, her heart singing antiphonally with the birds outside. Coatless, but capped and in her gray uniform, she jumped the hospital steps, two at a time, and danced the length of the street.

Now Margaret MacLean was small and slender, and there was nothing grotesque in the dancing. It had become a natural means of expressing the abundant life and joyousness she had felt ever since she had been free of crutches and wheeled chairs; and an impartial stranger, had he been passing, would have watched her with the same uncritical delight that he might have bestowed on any wood creature had it suddenly appeared darting along the pavement. She reached the corner just in time to bump into the flower-seller, who was turning about like some old tabby to settle himself and his basket.

"Oh!" she cried in dismay, for the flower-seller was wizened and unsteady of foot, and she had sent him spinning about in a dizzy fashion. She put out a steadying hand. "Oh . . . !" This time it was in ecstasy; she had spied the primroses in the basket just as the sunshine splashed over the edge of the corner building straight down upon them. Margaret MacLean dropped to one knee and laid her cheek against them. "The happy things—you can hear them laugh! I want all—all I can carry." She looked up quizzically at the flower-seller. "Now how did you ever happen to think of bringing these—to-day?"

A pair of watery old eyes twinkled, thereby becoming amazingly young in an instant, and he wagged his head mysteriously while he raised a significant finger. "Sure, wasn't I knowin', an' could I be afther bringin' anythin' else? But the rest that passes—or stops—will see naught but yellow flowers in a basket, I'm thinkin'." And the flower-seller set to shaking his head sorrowfully.

"Perhaps not. There are the children—"

"Aye, the childher; but the most o' them be's gettin' too terrible wise."

"I know—I know—but mine aren't. I'm going to take my children back as many as I can carry." She stretched both hands about a mass of stems—all they could compass. "See"—she held up a giant bunch—"so much happiness is worth a great deal. Feel in the pocket of my apron and you will find—gold for gold. It was the only money I had in my purse. Keep it all, please." With a nod and a smile she left him, dancing her way back along the still deserted street.

"'Tis the faeries' own day, afther all," chuckled the flower-seller as he eyed the tiny gold disk in his palm; then he remembered, and called after the diminishing figure of the nurse: "Hey, there! Mind what ye do wi' them blossoms. They be's powerful strong magic." And he chuckled again.

The hall-boy, shorn of uniform and dignity, was outside, polishing brasses, when Margaret MacLean reached the hospital door. She stopped for an interchange of grins and greetings.

"Mornin', Miss Peggie."

"Morning, Patsy."

He was "Patrick" to the rest of Saint Margaret's; no one else seemed to realize that he was only about one-fifth uniform and the other fifths were boy—small boy at that.

She eyed his work critically. "That's right—polish them well, Patsy. They must shine especially bright to-day."

"Why, what's happenin' to-day?"

"Oh—everything, and—nothing at all."

And she passed on through the door with a most mysterious smile, thereby causing Patsy to mentally comment:

"My, don't she beat all! More'n half the time a feller don't know what she's kiddin' about; but, gee! don't he like it!"

As it happened the primroses did not get as far as Ward C then. Margaret MacLean found the door of the board-room ajar, and, glancing in, looked square into the eyes of the Founder of Saint Margaret's, where he hung in his great gold frame—silent and questioning.

"If all the tales they tell about you are true, you must wonder what has happened to Saint Margaret's since you turned it over to a board of trustees."

She went in and stood close to him, smiling wistfully. "Perhaps you would like me to leave you the primroses until after the meeting—they would be sure to cheer you up; and they might—they might—" Laughing, she went over to the President's desk and put the flowers in the green Devonshire bowl.

She was sitting in the President's chair, coaxing some of the hoydenish blossoms into place, when the House Surgeon looked in a moment later.

"Hello! What are you doing? I thought you detested this room." He spoke in a teasing, big-brother way, while his eyes dwelt pleasurably on the small gray figure in the President's chair. For, be it said without partiality or prejudice, Margaret MacLean was beautiful, with a beauty altogether free from self-appraisement.

"I do—I hate it!" Then she wagged her head and raised a significant finger in perfect imitation of the flower-seller. "I am dabbling in—magic. I am starting here a terrible and insidious campaign against gloom."

The House Surgeon looked amused. "You make me shiver, all right; but I haven't the smallest guess coming. Would you mind putting it into scientific American?"

"I'm afraid I couldn't. But I can make a plain statement in prose—this is Trustee Day."

"Hell!" The House Surgeon walked over to the calendar on the desk to verify the fact. "Well, what are you going to do about it?"

Margaret MacLean spread her hands over the primroses, indicatively. "I told you—magic." She wrinkled up her forehead into a worrisome frown. "Let me see; I counted them, up last night, and I have had two hundred and twenty-eight Trustee Days in my life. I have tried about everything else—philosophy, Christianity, optimism, mental sclerosis, and missionary fever; but never magic. Don't you think it sounds—hopeful?"

The House Surgeon laughed. "You are the funniest little person I ever knew. On duty you're as old as Methuselah and as wise as Hippocrates, but the rest of the time I believe your feet are eternally treading the nap off antique wishing-carpets. I wonder how many you've worn out. As for that head of yours, it bobs like a penny balloon among the clouds looking for—"

"Faeries?" suggested Margaret MacLean.

"That just about hits it. Will you please tell me how you, of all people, ever evolved these—ideas—out of Saint Margaret's?"

A grim smile tightened the corners of her mouth while she looked across the room to the portrait that hung opposite the Founder's—the portrait of the Old Senior Surgeon. "I had to," she said at last. "When a person is born with absolutely nothing—nothing of the human things a human baby is entitled to—she has to evolve something to live in; a sort of sea-urchin affair with spines of make-believe sticking out all over it to keep prodding away life as it really is. If she didn't the things she had missed would flatten her out into a flabby pulp—just skin and feelings."

"And so you make believe that Trustee Day isn't really bad?"

"Oh dear, no! But I keep believing it's going to be much better. Did you ever think what it could be like—if the trustees would only make it something more than—a matter of business? Why, it could be as good as any faery-tale come true, with a dozen god-parents instead of one; and think of the wonderful things they could do it they tried. Think—think—and, oh, the fun of it!"

She broke off with a little shivering ache. When the picture became so alive that it pulled at one's heart-strings, it was time to stop. But the next moment she was laughing merrily.

"Do you know, when I was a little tad and couldn't sleep at night with the pain, I used to make believe I was a 'truster' and say over to myself all the nice, comforting things I wished they would say. It began to sound so real that one day I answered—just as if some one had said something pleasant."

"Well?" interrogated the House Surgeon, much amused.

"Well, it was the Oldest Trustee, of course; and she raised those lorgnettes and reminded me that a good child never spoke unless she was spoken to. I suppose it will take lots and lots of magic to turn them into god-parents."

"Look here," and the House Surgeon reached across the desk and took a firm, big-brother grip of her hands, "faery-tales have to have stepmothers as well as godmothers—think of it that way. And remember that those kiddies of yours were never born to ride in pumpkin coaches."

"But I'm not reaching out for faery luxuries for them. I want them to be children—plain, happy, laughing children—with as normal a heritage as we can scrape together for them. All it needs is the magic of a little human understanding. That's the most potent magic in the whole world. Why, it can do anything!"

A little-girl look came into Margaret MacLean's face. It always did when she was wanting anything very much or was thinking about something very intensely. It was the hardest kind of a look to resist. She had often threshed this subject out with the House Surgeon before; for it was her theory that when a body's material condition was rather poor and meager there was all the more reason for scraping together what one could of a spiritual heritage and living thereby.

"And don't you see," she had urged, at least a score of times, "if we could only teach all the cripples to let their minds run—free-limbed—over hilltops and pleasant places, their natures would never need to warp and wither after the fashion of their poor bodies. And the time to begin is in childhood, when the mind is learning to walk alone."

Usually the House Surgeon was easily convinced to the Margaret MacLean side of any argument; but this time, for reasons of his own, he turned an unsympathetic and stubborn ear. He was coming to believe very strongly that all this fanciful optimism was so much laughing-gas, with only a passing power, and when the effect wore off there would be the Dickens to pay. He did not want to see Margaret MacLean turn into a bitter-minded woman of the world—stripped of her trust and her dreams. He—all of them—had need of her as she was. Her belief in the ultimate good of things and persons, however, was beyond power of human achievement; and the surest cure for disappointments was to amputate all expectations. So the House Surgeon hardened his heart and became as professionally severe as he knew how to be.

"It's absolutely impossible to expect a group of incurable children in an institution to be made as normal and happy as other children. It can't be done. Those kiddies are up against a pretty hard proposition, I know; but the kindest thing you can do for them is to toughen them into not feeling—"

The nurse in charge of Ward C wrenched away her hands fiercely. "You're just like the Senior Surgeon. He thinks the whole dependent world—the sick and the poor and the incompetent—have no business with ideas or feelings of their own. He's always saying, 'Train it out of them; train it out of them; and it will make it easier for institutions to take care of them.' It's for ever the 'right of the strong' with him. Unless you are able to take care of yourself you are not entitled to the ordinary privileges of a human being."

"I'm not at all like the Senior Surgeon. I don't mean that, and you know it. What I am trying to make you understand is that these kiddies can't keep you always; some time they will have to learn to do without you. When that happens it will come tough on them. It would come tough on anybody; and the square thing for you to do is to stop being—so all-fired adorable." The House Surgeon flung back his head and marched out of the board-room, slamming the door.

Behind the slammed door Margaret MacLean eyed the primroses suspiciously. "I wonder—is your magic working all right to-day? Please—please don't weave any charms against him, little faery people. He is the only other grown-up person who has ever understood the least bit; and I couldn't bear to lose him, too."

For the second time that morning she nestled her cheek against the blossoms. Then the clock on the hospital tower struck eight. She jumped with a start. "Time to go on duty." Once again her eyes met the eyes of the Founder and sparkled witchingly. She raised high the green Devonshire bowl from the President's desk as for a toast.

"Here's to Saint Margaret's—as you founded her; and the children—as you meant them to be; and here's to the one who first understood!" She turned from the Founder to the portrait hanging opposite, and bowed most worshipfully to the Old Senior Surgeon.

II
IN WHICH MARGARET MACLEAN REVIEWS A MEMORY

As Margaret MacLean climbed the stairs to Ward C—she rarely took the lift, it was too remindful of the time when she could not climb stairs—her mind thought back a step for each step she mounted. When she had reached the top of the first flight she was a child again, back in one of the little white iron cribs in her own ward; and it was the day when the first stringent consciousness came to her that she hated Trustee Day.

The Old Senior Surgeon—the present one, of whom Saint Margaret's felt inordinately proud, was house surgeon then—had come into Ward C for a peep at her, and had called out, according to a firmly established custom, "Hello, Thumbkin! What's the news?"

She had been "Thumbkin" to him ever since the night he had carried her into the hospital, a tiny mite of a baby; and he had woven out of her coming a marvelous story—fancy-fashioned. This he had told her at least twice a week, from the time she was old enough to ask for it, because it had popped into his head quite suddenly that this morsel of humanity would some day insist on being accounted for.

The bare facts concerning her were rather shabby ones. She had been unceremoniously dumped into his arms by a delegate from the Foundling Asylum, who had found him the most convenient receptacle nearest the door; and he had been offered the meager information that she belonged to no one, was wrong somehow, and a hospital was the place for her.

One hardly likes to pass on shabby garments, much less shabby facts, to cover another's past. So the Old Senior Surgeon had forestalled her inquisitiveness with a tale adorned with all the pretty imaginings that he, "a clumsy-minded old gruffian," could conjure up.

Margaret MacLean remembered the story—word for word—as we remember "The House That Jack Built." It began with the Old Senior Surgeon himself, who heard a pair of birds disputing in one of the two trees which sentineled the hospital. They had built a nest therein; it was bedtime, and they wished to retire, only something prevented. Upon investigation he discovered the cause—"and there you were, my dear, no bigger than my thumb!"

This was the nucleus of the story; but the Old Senior Surgeon had rolled it about, hither and yon, adding adventure after adventure, until it had assumed gigantic proportions. As she grew older she took a hand in the adventure-making herself, he supplying the bare plot, she weaving the threads therefrom into a detailed narrative which she retold to him later, with a few imaginings of her own added. This is what had established the custom for the Old Senior Surgeon to take a peep into Ward C at day's end and call across to her: "Hello, Thumbkin! What's the news?" or, "What's happened next?" And until this day the answer had always been a joyous one.

Margaret MacLean, grown, could look back at tiny Margaret MacLean and see her very clearly as she straightened up in the little iron crib and answered in a shrill, tense voice: "I'm not Thumbkin. I'm a foundling. I don't belong to anybody. I never had any father or mother or nothing, but just a hurt back; they said so. They stood right there—two of them; and one told the other all about me."

This was the end of the story, and the beginning of Trustee Days for Margaret MacLean.

She soon made the discovery that she was not the only child in the ward who felt about it that way. Her discovery was a matter of intuition rather than knowledge; for—as if by silent consent—the topic was carefully avoided in the usual ward conversation. One does not make it a rule to talk about the hobgoblins that lurk in the halls at night, or the gray, creeping shapes that come out of dark corners and closets after one has gone to bed, if one is so pitifully unfortunate as to possess these things in childhood. Instead one just remembers and waits, shivering. Only to old Cassie, the scrub-woman, who was young Cassie then, did she confide her fear. From her she received a charm—compounded of goose eggshells and vinegar—which Cassie claimed to be what they used in Ireland to unbewitch changelings. She kept the charm hidden for months under her pillow. It proved comforting, although absolutely ineffectual.

And for months there had been a strained relationship between the Old Senior Surgeon and herself, causing them both much embarrassment. She resented the story he had made for her with all her child soul; he had cheated her—fooled her. She felt much as we felt toward our parents when we made our first discovery concerning Santa Claus.

But after a time—a long time—the story came to belong to her again; she grew to realize that the Old Senior Surgeon had told it truthfully—only with the unconscious tongue of the poet instead of the grim realist. She found out as well that it had done a wonderful thing for her: it had turned life into an adventure—a quest upon which one was bound to depart, no matter how poorly one's feet might be shod or how persistently the rain and wind bit at one's marrow through the rags of a conventional cloak. More than this—it had colored the road ahead for her, promising pleasant comradeship and good cheer; it would keep her from ever losing heart or turning back.

A day came at last when she and the Old Senior Surgeon could laugh—a little foolishly, perhaps—over the child-story; and then, just because they could laugh at it and feel happy, they told it together all over again. They made much of Thumbkin's christening feast, and the gifts the good godmothers brought.

"Let me see," said the Old Senior Surgeon, cocking his head thoughtfully, "there was the business-like little party on a broomstick, carrying grit—plain grit."

"And the next one brought happiness—didn't she?" asked little Margaret MacLean.

He nodded. "Of course. Then came a little gray-haired faery with a nosegay of Thoughts-for-other-folks, all dried and ready to put away like sweet lavender."

"And did the next bring love?"

Again he agreed. "But after her, my dear, came a comfortable old lady in a chaise with a market-basket full of common-sense."

"And then—then— Oh, couldn't the one after her bring beauty? Some one always did in the book stories. I think I wouldn't mind the back and—other things so much if my face could be nice."

Margaret MacLean, grown, could remember well how tearfully eager little Margaret MacLean had been.

The Old Senior Surgeon looked down with an odd, crinkly smile. "Have you never looked into a glass, Thumbkin?"

She shook her head.

Children in the wards of free hospitals have no way of telling how they look, and perhaps it is better that way. Only if it happens—as it does sometimes—that they spend a good share of their life there, it seems as if they never had a chance to get properly acquainted with themselves.

For a moment he patted her hand; after which he said, very solemnly: "Wait for a year and a day—then look. You will find out then just what the next faery brought."

Margaret MacLean had obeyed this command to the letter. When the year and a day came she had been able to stand on tiptoe and look at herself for the first time in her life; and she would never forget the gladness of that moment. It had appeared nothing short of a miracle to her that she should actually possess something of which she need not be ashamed—something nice to share with the world. And whenever Margaret MacLean thought of her looks at all, which was rare, she thought of them in that way.

She took up the memory again where she had dropped it on the second flight of stairs, slowly climbing her way to Ward C, and went on with the story.

They came to the place where Thumbkin was pricked by the wicked faery with the sleeping-thorn and put to sleep for a hundred years, after the fashion of many another story princess; and the Old Senior Surgeon suddenly stopped and looked at her sharply.

"Some day, Thumbkin, I may play the wicked faery and put you to sleep. What would you say to that?"

She did not say—then.

More months passed, months which brought an ashen, drawn look to the face of the Old Senior Surgeon, and a tired-out droop to his shoulders and eyes. She began to notice that the nurses eyed him pityingly whenever he came into the ward, and the house surgeon shook his head ominously. She wondered what it meant; she wondered more when he came at last to remind her of his threatened promise.

"You remember, Thumbkin, about that sleep? Would you let an old faery doctor put you to sleep, for a little while, if he was very sure you would wake up to find happiness—and health—and love—and all the other gifts the godmothers brought?"

She tried her best to keep the frightened look out of her eyes. By the way he watched her, however, she knew some of it must have crept in. "Operation?" she managed to choke out at last.

Operation was a fairly common word in Ward C, and not an over-hopeful one.

"It's this way, Thumbkin; and let's make a bargain of it. I think there's a cure for that back of yours. It hasn't been tried very much; about often enough to make it worth while for us to take a chance. I'll be honest with you and tell you the house surgeon doesn't think it can be done; but that's where the bargain comes in. He thinks he can mend my trouble, and I don't; and we're both dreadfully greedy to prove we're right. Now if you will give me my way with you I will give him his. But you must come first."

"A hundred years is a long time to be asleep," she objected.

"Bless you, it won't be a hundred minutes."

"And does your back need it, too?"

"Not my back; my stomach. It's about the only chance for either of us, Thumbkin."

"And you won't unless I do?"

The Old Senior Surgeon gave his head a terrific shake; then he caught her small hands in his great, warm, comforting ones. "Think. It means a strong back; a pair of sturdy little legs to take you anywhere; and the whole world before you!"

"And you'll have them, too?"

He smiled convincingly.

"All right. Let's." She gave his hand a hard, trustful squeeze.

She liked to remember that squeeze. She often wondered if it might not have helped him to do what he had to do.

Her operation was record-making in its success; and after he had seen her well on the mend he gave himself over to the house surgeon and a fellow-colleague, according to the bargain. He proved the house surgeon wrong, for he never rallied. Undoubtedly he knew this would be the way of it; for he stopped in Ward C before he went up to the operating-room and said to her:

"I shall be sleeping longer than you did, Thumbkin; but, never fear, I shall be waking some time, somewhere. And remember this: Never grow so strong and well that you forget how tiresome a hospital crib can be. Never be so happy that you grow blind to the heartaches of other children; and never wander so far away from Saint Margaret's that you can't come back, sometimes, and make a story for some one else."

She puzzled a good bit over this, especially the first part of it; but when they told her the next day, she understood. Probably she grieved for him more than had any one else; even more than the members of his own family or profession. For, whereas there are many people in the world who can give life to others, there are but few who can help others to possess it.

What childhood she had had she left behind her soon after this, along with her aching back, her helpless limbs, and the little iron crib in Ward C.

On the first Trustee Day following her complete recovery she appeared, at her own request, before the meeting of the board. In a small, frightened voice she asked them to please send her away to school. She wanted to learn enough to come back to Saint Margaret's and be a nurse.

The trustees consented. Having assumed the responsibility of her well-being for over fifteen years, they could not very easily shirk it now. Furthermore, was it not a praise-worthy tribute to Saint Margaret's as a charitable institution, and to themselves as trustees, that this child whom they had sheltered and helped to cure should choose this way of showing her gratitude? Verily, the board pruned and plumed itself well that day.

All this Margaret MacLean lived over again as she climbed the stairs to Ward C on the 30th of April, her heart glowing warm with the memory of this man who had first understood; who had freed her mind from the abnormality of her body and the stigma of her heritage; who had made it possible for her to live wholesomely and deeply; and who had set her feet upon a joyous mission. For the thousandth time she blessed that memory.

It had been no disloyalty on her part that she had closed her lips and said nothing when the House Surgeon had questioned her about her fancy-making. She could never get away from the feeling that some of the sweetness and sacredness might be lost with the telling of the memory. One is so apt to cheapen a thing when one tries hastily to put it into words, and ever afterward it is never quite the same.

On the second floor she stopped; and by chance she looked over, between spiral banisters, to the patch of hallway below. It just happened that the House Surgeon was standing there, talking with one of the internes.

Margaret MacLean smiled whimsically. "If there is a soul in the wide world I could share it with, it is the House Surgeon." And then she added, aloud, softly apostrophizing the top of his head, "I think some day you might grow to be very—very like the Old Senior Surgeon; that is, if you would only stop trying to be like the present one."

[Illustration: "If there is a soul in the wide world I could share it with, it is the House Surgeon."]

III
WARD C

A welcoming shout went up from Ward C as Margaret MacLean entered. It was lusty enough to have come from the throats of healthy children, and it would have sounded happily to the most impartial ears; to the nurse in charge it was a very pagan of gladness.

"Wish you good morning, good meals, and good manners," laughed Margaret MacLean; and then she went from crib to crib with a special greeting for each one. Oh, she firmly believed that a great deal depended on how the day began.

In the first crib lay Pancho, of South American parentage, partially paralyzed and wholly captivating. He had been in Saint Margaret's since babyhood—he was six now—and had never worn anything but a little hospital shirt.

"Good morning, Brown Baby," she said, kissing his forehead. "It's just the day for you out on the sun-porch; and you'll hear birds—lots of them."

"Wobins?"

"Yes, and bluebirds, too. I've heard them already."

Next came Sandy—merry of heart—a humpback laddie from Aberdeen. His parents had gone down with the steerage of a great ocean liner, and society had cared for him until the first horror of the tragedy had passed; then some one fortunately had mentioned Saint Margaret's, and society was relieved of its burden. In the year he had spent here his Aberdonian burr had softened somewhat and a number of American colloquialisms had crept into his speech; but for all that he was "the braw canny Scot"—as the House Surgeon always termed him—and he objected to kisses. So the good-morning greeting was a hearty hand-shake between the two—comrade fashion.

"It wad be a bonnie day i' Aberdeen," he reminded her, blithely. "But 'tis no the robins there 'at wad be singin'."

"Shall I guess?"

"Na, I'll tell ye. Laverocks!"

"Really, Sandy?" And then she suddenly remembered something. "Now you guess what you're going to have for supper to-night."

"Porridge?"

"No; scones!"

"Bully!" And Sandy clapped his hands ecstatically.

Beside Sandy lay Susan—smart, shrewd, and American, with braced legs and back, and a philosophy that failed her only on Trustee Days. But as calendars are not kept in Ward C no one knew what this day was; and consequently Susan was grinning all over her pinched, gnome-like little face. Margaret MacLean kissed her on both cheeks; the Susan-kind hunger for affection, but the world rarely finds it out and therefore gives sparingly.

"Guess yer couldn't guess what I dreamt last night, Miss Peggie?"

"About the aunt?" This was a mythical relation of Susan's who lived somewhere and who was supposed to turn up some day and claim Susan with open arms. She was the source of many dreams and of much interested conversation and heated argument in the ward, and the children had her pictured down to the smallest detail of person and clothes.

"No, 'tain't my aunt this time. I dreamt you was gettin' married, Miss Peggie." And Susan giggled delightedly.

"An' goin' away?" This was groaned out in chorus from the two cots following Susan's, wherein lay James and John—fellow-Apostles of pain—bound closely together in that spiritual brotherhood. They were sitting up, holding hands and staring at Margaret with wide, anguish-filled eyes.

"Of course I'm not going away, little brothers; and I'm not going to get married. Does any one ever get married in Saint Margaret's?"

The Apostles thought very hard about it for a moment; but as it had never happened before, of course it never would now, and Miss Peggie was safe.

The whole ward smiled again. But in that moment Margaret MacLean remembered what the House Surgeon had said, and wondered. Was she building up for them an ultimate discontent in trying to make life happy and full for them now? Could not minds like theirs be taught to walk alone, after all? And then she laughed to herself for worrying. Why should the children ever have to do without her—unless—unless something came to them far better—like Susan's mythical aunt? The children need never leave Saint Margaret's as long as they lived, and she never should; and she passed on to the next cot, content that all was well.

As she stooped over the bed a pair of thin little arms flew out and clasped themselves tightly about her neck; a head with a shock of red curls buried itself in the folds of the gray uniform. This was Bridget—daughter of the Irish sod, oldest of the ward, general caretaker and best beloved; although it should be added in justice to both Bridget and Margaret MacLean that the former had no consciousness of it, and the latter took great care to hide it.

[Illustration: As she stooped over the bed a pair of thin little arms flew out and clasped themselves tightly about her neck.]

It was Bridget who read to the others when no one else could; it was Bridget who remembered some wonderful story to tell on those days when Sandy's back was particularly bad or the Apostles grew over-despondent; and it was Bridget who laughed and sang on the gray days when the sun refused to be cheery. Undoubtedly it was because of all these things that her cot was in the center of Ward C.

Concerning Bridget herself, hers was a case of arsenical poisoning, slowly absorbed while winding daisy-stems for an East Broadway manufacturer of cheap artificial flowers. She had done this for three years—since she was five—thereby helping her mother to support themselves and two younger children. She was ten now and the Senior Surgeon had already reckoned her days.

In the shadow of Bridget's cot was Rosita's crib—Rosita being the youngest, the most sensitive, and the most given to homesickness. This last was undoubtedly due to the fact that she was the only child in the incurable ward blessed in the matter of a home. Her parents were honest-working Italians who adored her, but who were too ignorant and indulgent to keep her alive. They came every Sunday, and sat out the allotted time for visitors beside her crib, while the other children watched in a silent, hungry-eyed fashion.

Margaret MacLean passed her with a kiss and went on to Peter—Peter—seven years old—congenital hip disease—and all boy.

"Hello, you!" he shouted, squirming under the kiss that he would not have missed for anything.

"Hello, you!" answered back the administering nurse, and then she asked, solemnly, "How's Toby?"

"He's—he's fine. That soap the House Surgeon give me cured his fleas all up."

Toby was even more mythical than Susan's aunt; she was based on certain authentic facts, whereas Toby was solely the creation of a dog-adoring little brain. But no one was ever inconsiderate enough to hint at his airy fabrication; and Margaret MacLean always inquired after him every morning with the same interest that she bestowed on the other occupants of Ward C.

Last in the ward came Michael, a diminutive Russian exile with valvular heart trouble and a most atrocious vocabulary. The one seemed as incurable as the other. Margaret MacLean had wrestled with the vocabulary on memorable occasions—to no avail; and although she had long since discovered it was a matter of words and not meanings with him, it troubled her none the less. And because Michael came the nearest to being the black sheep of this sanitary fold she showed for him always an unfailing gentleness.

"Good morning, dear," she said, running her fingers through the perpendicular curls that bristled continuously.

"Goot mornun, tear," he mimicked, mischievously; and then he added, with an irresistible smile, "Und Got-tam-you."

"Oh, Michael, don't you remember, the next time you were going to say 'God bless you'?"

"Awright—next time."

Margaret MacLean sighed unconsciously. Michael's "next time" was about as reliable as the South American *mañana*; and he seemed as much an alien now as the day he was brought into the ward. And then, because she believed that kindness was the strongest weapon for victory in the end, she did the thing Michael loved best.

Ward C was turned into a circus menagerie, and Margaret MacLean and her assistant were turned into keepers. Together they set about the duties for the day with great good-humor. Two seals, a wriggling hippopotamus, a roaring polar bear, a sea-serpent of surprising activities, two teeth-grinding alligators, a walrus, and a baby elephant were bathed with considerable difficulty and excitement. It was Sandy who insisted on being the elephant in spite of a heated argument from the other animals that, having a hump, he ought to be a camel. They forgave him later, however, when he squirted forth his tooth-brush water and trumpeted triumphantly, thereby causing the entire menagerie to squirm about and bellow in great glee.

At this point the head keeper had to turn them all back instantly into children, and she delivered a firm but gentle lecture on the inconsiderateness of soaking a freshly changed bed.

Sandy broke into penitent tears; and because tears were never allowed to dampen the atmosphere of Ward C when they could possibly be dammed, Margaret MacLean did the "best-of-all-things." She pushed the cribs and cots all together into a "special" with observation-cars; then, changing into an engineer, and with a call to Toby to jump aboard, she swung herself into the caboose-rocker and opened the throttle. The bell rang; the whistle tooted; and the engine gave a final snort and puff, bounding away countryward where spring had come.

Those of you who live where you can always look out on pleasant places, or who can travel at will into them, may find it hard to understand how wearisome and stupid it grows to be always in one room with an encompassing sky-line of roof-tops and chimneys, or may fail to sound the full depths of wonder and delight over the ride that Ward C took that memorable day.

The engineer pointed out everything—meadows full of flowers, trees full of birds, gardens new planted, and corn-fields guarded by scarecrows. She slowed up at the barnyards that the children might hear the crowing cocks and clucking hens with their new-hatched broods, and see the neighboring pastures with their flocks of sheep and tiny lambs.

"A ken them weel—hoo the wee creepits bleeted hame i' Aberdeen!" shouted Sandy, bleeting for the whole pastureful.

And when they came to the smallest of mountain brooks the engineer followed it, down, down, until it had grown into a stream with cowslipped banks; and on and on until it had grown into a river with little boats and sandy shore and leaping fish. Here the engineer stopped the train; and every one who wanted to—and there were none who did not—went paddling; and some went splashing about just as if they could swim.

Back in the "special," they climbed a hilltop, slowly, so that the engineer could point out each farm and pasture and stream in miniature that they had seen close by.

"That's the wonder of a hilltop," she explained; "you can see everything neighboring each other." And when they reached the crest she clapped her hands. "Oh, children dear, wouldn't it be beautiful to build a house on a hilltop just like this to live in always!"

Afterward they rode into deep woods, where the sunlight came down through the trees like splashes of gold; and here the engineer suggested they should have a picnic.

As Margaret MacLean stepped out into the hall to look up the dinner-trays she met the House Surgeon.

"Dreading it as much as usual?" he asked, in the teasing, big-brother tone; but he looked at her in quite another way.

She laughed. "I'm hoping it isn't going to be as bad as the time before—and the time before that—and the time before that." She pushed back some moist curls that had slipped out from under her cap—engineering was hard work—and the little-girl look came into her face. She looked up mischievously at the House Surgeon. "You couldn't possibly guess what I've been doing all morning."

The House Surgeon wrinkled his forehead in his most professional manner. "Precautionary disinfecting?"

Margaret MacLean laughed again. "That's an awfully good guess, but it's wrong. I've been administering antitoxin for trusteria."

In spite of her gay assurance before the House Surgeon, however, it was rather a sober nurse in charge of Ward C who sat down that afternoon with a book of faery-tales on her knee open to the story of "The Steadfast Tin Soldier." As for Ward C, it was supremely happy; its beloved "Miss Peggie" was on duty for the afternoon with the favorite book for company; moreover, no one had discovered as yet that this was Trustee Day and that the trustees themselves were already near at hand.

A shadow fell athwart the threshold that very moment. Margaret MacLean could feel it without taking her eyes from the book, and, purposefully unmindful of its presence, she kept reading steadily on:

"'The paper boat was rocking up and down; sometimes it turned round so quickly that the Tin Soldier trembled; but he remained firm, he did not move a muscle, and looked straight forward, shouldering his musket.'"

"Ah, Miss MacLean, may I speak with you a moment?" It was the voice of the Meanest Trustee.

The nurse in charge rose quickly and met him half-way, hoping to keep him and whatever he might have to say as far from the children as possible.

The Meanest Trustee continued in a little, short, sharp voice: "The cook tells me that the patients in this ward have been having extra food prepared for them of late, such as fruit and jellies and scones and even ice-cream. I discovered it for myself. I saw some pineapples in the refrigerator when I was inspecting it this afternoon, and the cook said it was your orders."

Margaret MacLean smiled her most ingratiating smile. "You see," she said, eagerly, "the children in this ward get fearfully tired of the same things to eat; it is not like the other wards where the children stay only a short time. So I thought it would be nice to have something different—once in a while; and then the old things would taste all the better—don't you see? I felt sure the trustees would be willing."

"Well, they are not. It is an entirely unnecessary expense which I will not countenance. The regular food is good and wholesome, and the patients ought to feel grateful for it instead of finding fault."

The nurse looked anxiously toward the cots, then dropped her voice half an octave lower.

"The children have never found fault; it was just my idea to give them a treat when they were not expecting it. As for the extra expense, there has been none; I have paid for everything myself."

The Meanest Trustee readjusted his eye-glasses and looked closer at the young woman before him. "Do you mean to say you paid for them out of your own wages?"

The nurse nodded.

"Then all I have to say is that I consider it an extremely idiotic performance which had better be stopped. Children should not be indulged."

And he went away muttering something about the poor always remaining poor with their foolish notions of throwing away money; and Margaret MacLean went back to the book of faery-tales. But as she was looking for the place Sandy grunted forth stubbornly:

"A'm no wantin' ony scones the nicht, so ye maun na fetch them."

And Peter piped out, "Trusterday, ain't it, Miss Peggie?"

"Yes, dear. Now shall we go on with the story?"

She had read to where the rat was demanding the passport when she recognized the President's step outside the door. In another moment he was standing beside her chair, looking at the book on her knee.

"Humph! faery-tales! Is that not very foolish? Don't you think, Miss Margaret, it would be more suitable to their condition in life if you should select—hmm—something like *Pilgrim's Progress* or *Lives of the Saints and Martyrs*? Something that would be a preparation—so to speak—for the future." He stood facing her now, his back to the children.

"Excuse me"—she was smiling up at him—"but I thought this was a better preparation."

The President frowned. He was a much-tried man—a man of charitable parts, who directed or presided over thirty organizations. It took him nearly thirty days each month—with the help of two private secretaries and a luxurious office—to properly attend to all the work resulting therefrom; and the matters in hand were often so trying and perplexing that he had to go abroad every other year to avoid a nervous breakdown.

"I think we took up this matter at one of the business meetings," he went on, patiently, "and some arrangement was made for one of the trustees to come and read the Bible and teach the children their respective creeds and catechisms."

Margaret MacLean nodded. "There was; Miss N———"—and she named the Youngest and Prettiest Trustee—"generally comes an hour before the meeting and reads to them; but to-day she was detained by a—tango tea, I believe. That's why I chose this." Her eyes danced unconsciously as she tapped the book.

The President looked at her sharply. "I should think, my dear young lady, that you, of all persons, would realize what a very serious thing life is to any one in this condition. Instead of that I fear at times that you are—shall I say—flippant?" He turned about and looked at the children. "How do you do?" he asked, kindly.

"Thank you, sir, we are very well, sir," they chorused in reply. Saint Margaret's was never found wanting in politeness.

The President left; and the nurse in charge of Ward C went on with the reading.

"'The Tin Soldier stood up to his neck in water; deeper and deeper sank the boat, and the paper became more and more limp; then the water closed over him; but the Tin Soldier remained firm and shouldered his musket.'"

A group filled the doorway; it was the voice of the Oldest Trustee that floated in. "This, my dear, is the incurable ward; we are very much interested in it."

They stood just over the threshold—the Oldest Trustee in advance, her figure commanding and unbent, for all her seventy years, and her lorgnette raised. As she was speaking a little gray wisp of a woman detached herself from the group and moved slowly down the row of cots.

"Yes," continued the Oldest Trustee, "we have two cases of congenital hip disease and three of spinal tuberculosis—that is one of them in the second crib." Her eyes moved on from Sandy to Rosita. "And the fifth patient has such a dreadful case of rheumatism. Sad, isn't it, in so young a child? Yes, the Senior Surgeon says it is absolutely incurable."

Margaret MacLean closed the book with a bang; for five minutes the children had been looking straight ahead with big, conscious eyes, hearing not a word. Rebellion gripped at her heart and she rose quickly and went over to the group.

"Wouldn't you like to come in and talk to the children? They are rather sober this afternoon; perhaps you could make them laugh."

"Yes, wouldn't you like to go in?" put in the Oldest Trustee. "They are very nice children."

But the visitors shrank back an almost infinitesimal distance; and one said, hesitatingly:

"I'm afraid we wouldn't know quite what to say to them."

"Perhaps you would like to see the new pictures for the nurses' room?" the nurse in charge suggested, wistfully.

The Oldest Trustee glanced at her with a hint of annoyance. "We have already seen them. I think you must have forgotten, my dear, that it was I who gave them."

With flashing cheeks Margaret MacLean fled from Ward C. If she had stayed long enough to watch the little gray wisp of a woman move quietly from cot to cot, patting each small hand and asking, tenderly, "And what is your name, dearie?" she might have carried with her a happier feeling. At the door of the board-room she ran into the House Surgeon.

"Is it as bad as all that?" he asked after one good look at her.

"It's worse—a hundred times worse!" She tossed her head angrily. "Do you know what is going to happen some day? I shall forget who I am—and who they are and what they have done for me—and say things they will never forgive. My mind-string will just snap, that's all; and every little pestering, forbidden thought that has been kicking its heels against self-control and sense-of-duty all these years will come tumbling out and slip off the edge of my tongue before I even know it is there."

"They are some hot little thoughts, I wager," laughed the House Surgeon.

And then, from the far end of the cross-corridor, came the voice of the Oldest Trustee, talking to the group:

". . . such a very sweet girl—never forgets her place or her duty. She was brought here from the Foundling Asylum when she was a baby, in almost a dying condition. Every one thought it was an incurable case; the doctors still shake their heads over her miraculous recovery. Of course it took years; and she grew up in the hospital."

With a look of dumb, battling anger the nurse in charge of Ward C turned from the House Surgeon—her hands clenched—while the voice of the Oldest Trustee came back to them, still exhibiting:

"No, we have never been able to find out anything about her parentage; undoubtedly she was abandoned. We named her 'Margaret MacLean,' after the hospital and the superintendent who was here then. Yes, indeed—a very, very sad—"

When the Oldest Trustee reached the boardroom it was empty, barring the primroses, which were guilelessly nodding in the green Devonshire bowl on the President's desk.

IV
CURABLES AND INCURABLES

No one who entered the board-room that late afternoon remembered that it was May Eve; and even had he remembered, it would have amounted to nothing more than the mental process of association. It would not have given him the faintest presentiment that at that very moment the Little People were busy pressing their cloth-o'-dream mantles and reblocking their wishing-caps; that the instant the sun went down the spell would be off the faery raths, setting them free all over the world, and that the gates of Tir-na-n'Og would be open wide for mortals to wander back again. No, not one of the board remembered; the trustees sat looking straight at the primroses and saw nothing, felt nothing, guessed nothing.

They were not unusual types of trustees who served on the board of Saint Margaret's. You could find one or more of them duplicated in the directors' book of nearly any charitable institution, if you hunted for them; the strange part was, perhaps, that they were gathered together in a single unit of power. Besides the Oldest and the Meanest Trustees, there were the Executive, the Social, the Disagreeable, the Busiest, the Dominating, the Calculating, the Petty, and the Youngest and Prettiest. She came fluttering in a minute late from her tea; and right after her came the little gray wisp of a woman, who sat down in a chair by the door so unpretentiously as to make it appear as though she did not belong among them. When the others saw her they nodded distantly: they had just been talking about her.

It seemed that she was the widow of the Richest Trustee. The board had elected her to fill her husband's place lest the annual check of ten thousand—a necessary item on Saint Margaret's books—might not be forthcoming; and this was her first meeting. It was, in fact, her first visit to the hospital. She could never bear to come during her husband's trusteeship because, children having been denied her, she had wished to avoid them wherever and whenever she could, and spare herself the pain their suggestion always brought her. She would not have come now, but that her husband's memory seemed to require it of her.

For years gossip had been busy with the wife of the Richest Trustee—as the widow she did not relax her hold. What the trustees said that day they only repeated from gossip: the little gray wisp of a woman was a nonentity—nothing more—with the spirit of a mouse. She held no position in society, and what she did with her time or her money no one knew. The trustees smiled inwardly and reckoned silently with themselves; at least they would never need to fear opposition from her on any matter of importance.

The last person of all to enter the boardroom was the Senior Surgeon. The President had evidently waited for him, for he nodded to the House Surgeon to close the doors the moment he came.

Now the Senior Surgeon was a man who used capitals for Surgery, Science, and Self, unconsciously eliminating them elsewhere. He had begun in Saint Margaret's as house surgeon; and he had grown to be considered by many of his own profession the leading man of his day. The trustees were as proud of him as they were of the hospital, and it has never been recorded in the traditions of Saint Margaret's that the Senior Surgeon had ever asked for anything that went ungranted. He seldom attended a board meeting; consequently when he came in at five-thirty there was an audible rustle of excitement and the raising of anticipatory eyebrows.

When the President called the meeting to order every trustee was present, as well as the heads of the four wards, the Superintendent, and the two surgeons. The Senior Surgeon sat next to the President; the House Surgeon sat where he could watch equally well the profiles of the Youngest and Prettiest Trustee and Margaret MacLean. His heart had always been inclined to intermit; or—as he put it to himself—he adored them both in quite opposite ways; and which way was the better and more endurable he had never been able to decide.

"In view of the fact," said the President, rising, "that the Senior Surgeon can be with us but a short time this afternoon, and that he has a grave and vital issue to present to you, we will postpone the regular reports until the end of the meeting and take up at once the business in hand." He paused a moment, feeling the dramatic value of his next remark. "For some time the Senior Surgeon has seriously questioned the—hmm—advisability of continuing the incurable ward. He wishes very much to bring the matter before you, and he is prepared to give you his reasons for so doing. Afterward, I think it would be wise for us to discuss the matter very informally." He bowed to the Senior Surgeon and sat down.

The Meanest Trustee snapped his teeth together in an expression of grim satisfaction. "That ward is costing a lot of unnecessary expense, I think," he barked out, sharply, "and it's being run with altogether too free a hand." And he looked meaningly toward Margaret MacLean.

No one paid any particular attention to his remark; they were too deeply engrossed in the Senior Surgeon. And the House Surgeon, watching, saw the profile of the Youngest and Prettiest Trustee become even prettier as it blushed and turned in witching eagerness toward the man who was rising to address the meeting. The other profile had turned rigid and white as a piece of marble.

Now the Senior Surgeon could do a critical major operation in twenty minutes; and he could operate on critical issues quite as rapidly. Speed was his creed; therefore he characteristically attacked the subject in hand without any prefatory remarks.

"Ladies and gentlemen of the board, the incurable ward is doing nothing. I can see no possible reason or opportunity for further observation or experimentation there. Every case in it at the present time, as well as every Case that is likely to come to us, is as a sealed document as far as science is concerned. They are incurable—they will remain incurable for all time."

"How do you know?" The question came from the set lips of the nurse in charge of Ward C.

"How do we know anything in science? We prove it by undeniable, irrevocable facts."

"Even then you are not sure of it. I was proved incurable—but I got well."

"That proves absolutely nothing!" And the Senior Surgeon growled as he always did when things went against his liking. "You were a case in a thousand—in a lifetime. Because it happened once—here in this hospital—is no reason for believing that it will ever happen again."

"Oh yes, it is!" persisted Margaret MacLean. "There is just as much reason for believing as for not believing. Every one of those children, in the ward now might—yes, they might—be a case in a thousand; and no one has any right to take that thousandth of a chance away from them."

"You are talking nonsense—stupid, irrational nonsense." And the Senior Surgeon glared at her.

The truth was that he had never forgiven her for getting well. To have had a slip of a girl juggle with the most reliable of scientific data, as well as with his own undeniable skill as a diagnostician, and grow up normally, healthfully perfect, was insufferable. He had never quite forgiven the Old Senior Surgeon for his share in it. And to have her stand against him and his great desire, now, and actually throw this thing in his face, was more than he could endure. He did not know that Margaret MacLean was fighting for what she loved most on earth, the one thing that seemed to belong to her, the thing that had been given into her keeping by the right of a memory bequeathed to her by the man he could not save. Truth to tell, Margaret MacLean had never quite forgiven the Senior Surgeon for this, blameless as she knew him to be.

And so for the space of a quick breath the two faced each other, aggressive and accusing.

When the Senior Surgeon turned again to the President and the trustees his face wore a faint smile suggestive of amused toleration.

"I hope the time will soon come," he said very distinctly, "when every training-school for nurses will bar out the so-called sentimental, imaginative type; they do a great deal of harm to the profession. As I was saying, the incurable ward is doing nothing, and we need it for surgical cases. Look over the reports for the last few months and you will see how many cases we have had to turn away—twenty in March, sixteen in February; and this month it is over thirty—one a day. Now why waste that room for no purpose?"

"Every one of those cases could get into, some of the other hospitals; but who would take the incurables? What would you do with the children in Ward C, now?" and Margaret MacLean's voice rang out its challenge.

The Senior Surgeon managed to check an angry explosive and turned to the President for succor.

"I think," said that man of charitable parts, "that the meeting is getting a trifle too informal for order. After the Senior Surgeon has finished I will call on those whom I feel have something of—hmm—importance to say. In the mean time, my dear young lady, I beg of you not to interrupt again. The children, of course, could all be returned to their homes."

"Oh no, they couldn't—" There was something hypnotic in the persistence of the nurse in charge of Ward C.

Usually keenly sensitive, abnormally alive to impressions and atmosphere, she shrank from ever intruding herself or her opinions where they were not welcome; but now all personal consciousness was dead. She was wholly unaware that she had worked the Senior Surgeon into a state where he had almost lost his self-control—a condition heretofore unknown in the Senior Surgeon; that she had exasperated the President and reduced the trustees to open-mouthed amazement. The lorgnette shook unsteadily in the hand of the Oldest; and, unmindful of it all, Margaret MacLean went steadily on:

"Most of them haven't any homes, and the others couldn't live in theirs a month. You don't know how terrible they are—five families in one garret, nothing to eat some of the time, father drunk most of the time, and filth and foul air all of the time. That's the kind of homes they have—if they have any."

Her outburst was met with a complete silence, ignoring and humiliating. After a moment the Senior Surgeon went on, as if no one had spoken.

"Am I not right in supposing that you wish to further, as far as it lies within your power, the physical welfare and betterment of the poor in this city? That you wish to do the greatest possible good to the greatest number of children? Ah! I thought so. Well, do you not see how continuing to keep a number of incurable cases for two or three years—or as long as they live—is hindering this? You are keeping out so many more curable cases. For every case in that ward now we could handle ten or fifteen surgical cases each year. Is that not worth considering?"

The trustees nodded approval to one another; it was as if they would say, "The Senior Surgeon is always right."

The surgeon himself looked at his watch; he had three minutes left to clinch their convictions. Clearly and admirably he outlined his present scope of work; then, stepping into the future, he showed into what it might easily grow, had it the room and beds. He showed indisputably what experimental surgery had done for science—what a fertile field it was; and wherein lay Saint Margaret's chance to plow a furrow more and reap its harvest. At the end he intimated that he had outgrown his present limited conditions there, that unless these were changed he should have to betake himself and his operative skill elsewhere.

A painfully embarrassing hush closed in on the meeting as the Senior Surgeon resumed his seat. It was broken by an enthusiastic chirp from the Youngest and Prettiest Trustee. She had never attempted to keep her interest for him concealed in the bud, causing much perturbation to the House Surgeon, and leading the Disagreeable Trustee to remark, frequently:

"Good Lord! She'll throw herself at his head until he loses consciousness, and then she'll marry him."

"I think," said she, beaming in the direction of the Senior Surgeon, "that it would be perfectly wonderful to be the means of discovering some great new thing in surgery. And as our own great surgeon has just said, it is really ridiculous to let a few perfectly incurable cases stand in the way of science."

The House Surgeon looked from the beaming profile to the tense, drawn outline of mouth and chin belonging to the nurse in charge of Ward C, and he found himself wondering if art had ever pictured a crucified Madonna, and, if so, why it had not taken Margaret MacLean as a model. That moment the President called his name.

[Illustration: The House Surgeon looked from the beaming profile to the tense, drawn outline of mouth and chin belonging to the nurse in charge of Ward C.]

The House Surgeon was still young and unspoiled enough to blush whenever he was consulted. Moreover, he hated to speak in public, knowing, as he did, that he lacked the cultured manner and the polished speech of the Senior Surgeon. He always crawled out of it whenever he could, putting some one else more ready of tongue in his place. He was preparing to crawl this time when another look at the white profile in front of him brought him to his feet.

"See here," he burst out, bluntly, "we all know the chief is as clever as any surgeon in the country, and that he can do anything in the world he sets out to do, even to turning Saint Margaret's into a surgical laboratory. But you ought to stop him—you've got to stop him—that is your business as trustees of this institution. We don't need any more surgical laboratories just yet—they are getting along fast enough at Rockefeller, Johns Hopkins, and the Mayo clinic. What we scientific chaps need to remember—and it ought to be hammered at us three times a day, and then some—is that humanity was never put into the world for the sole purpose of benefiting science. We are apt to forget this and get to thinking that a few human beings more or less don't count in the face of establishing one scientific fact."

He paused just long enough to snatch a breath, and then went racing madly on. "Institutions are apt to forget that they are taking care of the souls and minds of human beings as well as their bodies. It seems to me that the man who founded this hospital intended it for humane rather than scientific purposes. His wishes ought to be considered now; and I wager he would say, if he were here, to let science go hang and keep the incurables."

The House Surgeon sat down, breathing heavily and mopping his forehead. It was the longest speech he had ever made, and he was painfully conscious of its inadequacy. The Senior Surgeon excused himself and left the room, not, however, until he had given the House Surgeon a look pregnant with meaning; Saint Margaret's would hardly be large enough to hold them both after the 30th of April.

The trustees moved restlessly in their chairs. The unexpected had happened; there was an internal rupture at Saint Margaret's; and for forty years the trustees had boasted of its harmonious behavior and kindly feelings. In a like manner do those dwellers in the shadow of a volcano continue to boast of their safety and the harmlessness of the crater up to the very hour of its eruption. And all the while the gray wisp of a woman by the door sat silent, her hands still folded on her lap.

At last the President rose; he coughed twice before speaking. "I think we will call upon the hospital committee now for their reports. Afterward we will take up the question of the incurable ward among the trustees—hmm—alone."

Every one sat quietly, almost listlessly, during the reading until Margaret MacLean rose, the report for Ward C in her hand. Then there came a raising of heads and a stiffening of backs and a setting of chins. She was very calm, the still calm of the China Sea before a typhoon strikes it; when she had finished reading she put the report on the chair back of her and faced the President with clasped hands and—a smile.

"It's funny," she said, irrelevantly, "for the first time in my life I am not afraid here."

And the House Surgeon muttered, under his breath: "Great guns! That mind-string has snapped."

"There is more to the report than I had the courage to write down when I was making it out; but I can give it very easily now, if you will not mind listening a little longer. You have always thought that I came back to Saint Margaret's because I felt grateful for what you had done for me—for the food and the clothes and the care, and later for the education that you paid for. This isn't true. I am grateful—very grateful—but it is a dutiful kind of gratitude which wouldn't have brought me back in a thousand years. I am so sorry to feel this way. Perhaps I would not if, in all the years that I was here as a child, one of you had shown me a single personal kindness, or some one had thought to send me a letter or a message while I was away at school. No, you took care of me because you thought it was your duty, and I am grateful for the same reason; but it was quite another thing which brought me back to Saint Margaret's."

The smile had gone; she was very sober now. And the House Surgeon, still watching the two profiles, suddenly felt his heart settle down to a single steady beat. He wanted to get up that very instant and tell the nurse in charge of Ward C what had happened and what he thought of her; but instead he dug his hands deep in his pockets. How in the name of the seven continents had he never before realized that she was the sweetest, finest, most adorable, and onliest girl in the world, and worth a whole board-room full of youngest and prettiest trustees?

"I came back," went on Margaret MacLean, slowly, "really because of the Old Senior Surgeon, to stand, as he stood in the days long ago, between you and the incurable ward; to shut out—if I could—the little, thoughtless, hurting things that you are always saying without being in the least bit conscious of them, and to keep the children from wanting too much the friendship and loving interest that, somehow, they expected from you. I wanted to try and make them feel that they were not case this and case that,

- 32 -

abnormally diseased and therefore objects of pity and curiosity to be pointed out to sympathetic visitors, but children—just children—with a right to be happy and loved. I wanted to fill their minds so full of fun and make-believe that they would have to forget about their poor little bodies. I tried to make you feel this and help without putting it—cruelly—into words; but you would never understand. You have never let them forget for a moment that they are 'incurables,' any more than you have let me forget that I am a—foundling."

She stopped a moment for breath, and the smile came back—a wistfully pleading smile. "I am afraid that last was not in the report. What I want to say is—please keep the incurable ward; take the time to really know them—and love them a little. If you only could you would never consider sending them away for a moment. And if, in addition to the splendid care you have given their bodies, you would only help to keep their minds and hearts sound and sweet, and shield them against curious visitors, why—why—some of them might turn out to be 'a case in a thousand.' Don't you see—can't you see—that they have as much right to their scraps of life and happiness—as your children have to their complete lives, and that there is no place for them anywhere if Saint Margaret's closes her doors?"

With an overwhelming suddenness she became conscious of the attitude of the trustees. She, who was nothing but a foundling and a charity patient herself, had dared to pass judgment on them; it was inconceivable—it was impertinent—it was beyond all precedent. Only the gray wisp of a woman sat silent, seeming to express nothing. Margaret MacLean's cheeks flamed; she shrank into herself, her whole being acutely alive to their thoughts. The scared little-girl look came into her face.

"Perhaps—perhaps," she stammered, pitifully, "after what I have said you would rather I did not stay on—in charge of Ward C?"

The Dominating Trustee rose abruptly. "Mr. President, I suggest that we act upon Miss MacLean's resignation at once."

"I second the motion," came in a quick bark from the Meanest Trustee, while the Oldest Trustee could be heard quoting, "Sharper than a serpent's tooth—"

The Executive Trustee rose, looking past Margaret MacLean as he spoke. "In view of the fact that we shall possibly discontinue the incurable ward, and that Miss MacLean seems wholly unsatisfied with our methods and supervision here, I motion that her resignation be accepted now, and that she shall be free to leave Saint Margaret's when her month shall have expired,"

"I second the motion," came from the Social Trustee, while she added to the Calculating, who happened to be sitting next: "So ill-bred. It just shows that a person can never be educated above her station in life."

The President rose. "The motion has been made and seconded. Will you please signify by raising your hands if it is your wish that Miss MacLean's resignation be accepted at once?"

Hand after hand went up. Only the little gray wisp of a woman in the chair by the door sat with her hands still folded on her lap.

"It is, so to speak, a unanimous vote." There was a strong hint of approval in the President's voice. He was a good man; but he belonged to that sect which holds as one of the main articles of its faith, "I believe in the infallibility of the rich."

"Can any one tell me when Miss MacLean's time expires?"

The person under discussion answered for herself. "On the last day of the month, Mr. President."

"Oh, very well." He was extremely polite in his manner. "We thank you for your very full and—hmm—comprehensive report. After to-night you are excused from your duties at Saint Margaret's."

The President bowed her courteously out of the board-room, while the primroses in the green Devonshire bowl on his desk still nodded guilelessly.

V
ODDS AND ENDS

Margaret MacLean walked the length of the first corridor; once out of sight and hearing, she tore up the stairs, her cheeks crimson and her eyes suspiciously moist. Before she had reached the second flight the House Surgeon overtook her.

"I wish," he panted behind her, trying his best to look the big-brother way of old—"I wish you'd wait a moment. This habit of yours of always walking up is a beastly one."

"Don't worry about it." There was a sharp, metallic ring in her voice that made it unnatural. "That's one habit that will soon be broken."

The House Surgeon smiled rather helplessly; inside he was making one of the few prayers of his life—a prayer to keep Margaret MacLean free of bitterness. "There is something I want to say to you," he began.

She broke in feverishly: "No, there isn't! And I don't want to hear it. I don't want to hear you're sorry. I don't want to hear they'll be taken care of—somewhere—somehow. I think I should scream if you told me it was bound to happen—or will all turn out for the best."

"I had no intention of saying any of those things—in fact, they hadn't even entered my mind. What I was going to—"

"Oh, I know. You were going to remind me of what you said this morning. Almost prophetic, wasn't it?" And there was a strong touch of irony in her laugh. She turned on him crushingly. "Perhaps you knew it all along. Perhaps it was your way of letting me down gently."

"See here," said the House Surgeon, bluntly, "that's the second disagreeable thing you've said to-day. I don't think it's quite square. Do you?"

"No!" Her lips quivered; her hands reached out toward his impulsively. "I don't know why I keep saying things I know are not true. I'm perfectly—unforgivably horrid."

As impulsively he took both hands, turned them palm uppermost, and kissed them.

[Illustration: Impulsively he took both hands, turned them palm uppermost, and kissed them.]

She snatched them away; the crimson in her cheeks deepened. "Don't, please. Your pity only makes it harder. Oh, I don't know what has happened—here—" And she struck her breast fiercely. "If—if they send the children away I shall never believe in anything again; the part of me that has believed and trusted and been glad will stop—it will break all to pieces." With a hard, dry sob she left him, running up the remaining stairs to Ward C. She did not see his arms reach hungrily after her or the great longing in his face.

The House Surgeon turned and went downstairs again.

In the lower corridor he ran across the President, who was looking for him. With much courtesy and circumlocution he was told the thing he had been waiting to hear: the board, likewise, had discovered that Saint Margaret's had suddenly grown too small to hold both the Senior Surgeon and himself. Strangely enough, this troubled him little; there are times in a man's life when even the most momentous of happenings shrink into nothing beside the simple process of telling the girl he loves that he loves her.

The President was somewhat startled by the House Surgeon's commonplace acceptance of the board's decision; and he returned to the board-room distinctly puzzled.

Meanwhile Margaret MacLean, having waited outside of Ward C for her cheeks to cool and her eyes to dry, opened the door and went in.

Ward C had been fed by the assistant nurse and put to bed; that is, all who could limp or wheel themselves about the room were back in their cribs, and the others were no longer braced or bolstered up. As she had expected, gloom canopied every crib and cot; beneath, eight small figures, covered to their noses, shook with held-back sobs or wailed softly. According to the custom that had unwittingly established itself, Ward C was crying itself to sleep. Not that it knew what it was crying about, it being merely a matter of atmosphere and unstrung nerves; but that is cause enough to turn the mind of a sick child all awry, twisting out happiness and twisting in peevish, fretful feelings.

She stood by the door, unnoticed, looking down the ward. Pancho lay wound up in his blanket like a giant chrysalis, rolling in silent misery. Sandy was stretched as straight and stiff as if he had been "laid out"; his eyes were closed, and there was a stolid, expressionless set to his features. Margaret MacLean knew that it betokened much internal disturbance. Susan, ex-philosopher, was sobbing aloud, pulling with rebellious fingers at the pieces of iron that kept her head where nature had planned it. The Apostles gripped hands and moaned in unison, while Peter hugged his blanket, seeking thereby some consolation for the dispelled Toby. Toby persistently refused to be conjured up on Trustee Days.

Only Bridget was alert and watchful. One hand was slipped through the bars of Rosita's crib, administering comforting pats to the rhythmic croon of an Irish reel. Every once in a while her eyes would wander to the neighboring cots with the disquiet of an over-troubled mother; the only moments of real unhappiness or worry Bridget ever knew were those which brought sorrow to the ward past her power of mending.

To Margaret MacLean, standing there, it seemed unbearable—as if life had suddenly become too sinister and cruel to strike at souls so little and helpless as these. There were things one could never explain in terms of God. She found herself wondering if that was why the Senior Surgeon worshiped science; and she shivered.

The room had become repellent; it was a sepulchral place entombing all she had lost. In the midst of the dusk and gloom her mind groped about—after its habit—for something cheerful, something that would break the colorless monotone of the room and change the atmosphere. In a flash she remembered the primroses; and the remembrance brought a smile.

"They're nothing but charlatans," she thought, "but the children will never find that out, and they'll be something bright for them to wake up to in the morning."

This was what sent her down the stairs again, just as the board meeting adjourned.

Now the board adjourned with thumbs down—signifying that the incurable ward was no more, as far as the future of Saint Margaret's was concerned. The trustees stirred in their chairs with a comfortable relaxing of joint and muscle, as if to say, "There, that is a piece of business well despatched; nothing like methods of conservation and efficiency, you know." Only the little gray wisp of a woman by the door sat rigid, her hands still folded on her lap.

The Oldest Trustee had just remarked to the Social Trustee that all the things gossip had said of the widow of the Richest Trustee were undoubtedly true—she was a nonentity—when the Senior Surgeon dropped in. This was according to the President's previous request. That gentleman of charitable parts had implied that there would undoubtedly be good news and congratulations awaiting him. This did not mean that the board intended to slight its duty and fail to consider the matter of the incurables with due conscientiousness—the board was as strong for conscience as for conservation. It merely went to show that the fate of Ward C had been preordained from the beginning; and that the President felt wholly justified in requesting the presence of the Senior Surgeon at the end of the meeting.

His appearance called forth such a laudatory buzzing of tongues and such a cordial shaking of hands that one might have easily mistaken the meeting for a successful political rally or a religious revival. The Youngest and Prettiest Trustee fluttered about him, chirping ecstatic expletives, while the Disagreeable Trustee watched her and growled to himself.

"So splendid," she chirped, "the unanimous indorsement of the board—at least, practically unanimous." And she eyed the widow of the Richest Trustee accusingly.

"The incurable ward and Margaret MacLean have really been a terrible responsibility, haven't they? I can't help feeling it will mean quite a load off our minds." It was the Social Trustee who spoke, and she followed it with a little sigh of relief.

The sigh was echoed twice—thrice—about the room. Then the Meanest Trustee barked out:

"I hope it will mean a load off our purses. That ward and that nurse have always wanted things, and had them, that they had no business wanting. I hope we can save a substantial sum now for the endowment fund."

The Oldest Trustee smiled tolerantly. "Of course it isn't as if the cases were not hopeless. I can see no object, however, in making concessions and sacrifices to keep in the hospital cases that cannot be cured; and, no doubt, we can place them most satisfactorily in state institutions for orphans or deficients."

At that moment the Youngest and Prettiest Trustee spied the primroses on the President's desk—she had been too engrossed in the surgical profession to observe much apart. "I believe I'm going to decorate you." And she dimpled up at the Senior Surgeon, coquettishly. Selecting one of the blossoms with great care, she drew it through the buttonhole in his lapel. "See, I'm decorating you with the Order of the Golden Primrose—for brilliancy." Whereupon she dropped her eyes becomingly.

"Good Lord!" muttered the Disagreeable Trustee to the President, his eye focused on the two. "She'll fetch him this time. And she'll have him so hypnotized with all this chirping and dancing business that he'll be perfectly helpless in a month, or I miss—"

The Youngest and Prettiest Trustee looked up just in time to intercept that eye, and she attacked it with a saucy little stare. "I believe you are both jealous," she flung over her shoulder. But the very next moment she was dimpling again. "I believe I am going to decorate everybody—including myself. I'm sure we all deserve it for our loyal support of Science." She, likewise, always spelled it with a capital, having acquired the habit from the Senior Surgeon.

She snatched a cluster of primroses from the green Devonshire bowl; and one was fastened securely in the lapel or frill of every trustee, not even omitting the gray wisp of a woman by the door.

And so it came to pass that every member of the board of Saint Margaret's Free Hospital for Children went home on May Eve with one of the faeries' own flowers tucked somewhere about his or her person. Moreover, they went home at precisely three minutes and twenty-two seconds past seven by the clock on the tower—the astronomical time for the sun to go down on the 30th of April. Crack went all the combination locks on all the faery raths, spilling the Little People over all the world; and creak went the gates of Tir-na-n'Og, swinging wide open for wandering mortals to come back.

As the trustees left the hospital the Senior Surgeon turned into the cross-corridor for his case, still gay with his Order of the Golden Primrose; and there, at the foot of the stairs, he ran into Margaret MacLean. They faced each other for the merest fraction of a breath, both conscious and embarrassed; then she glimpsed the flower in his coat and a cry of surprise escaped her.

He smiled, almost foolishly. "I thought they—it—looked rather pretty and—spring-like," he began, by way of explanation. His teeth ground together angrily; he sounded absurd, and he knew it. Furthermore, it was inexcusable of her to corner him in this fashion.

Now Margaret MacLean knew well enough that he would never have discovered the prettiness of anything by himself—not in a century of springtimes, and she sensed the truth.

"Did she decorate you?" she inquired, with an irritating little curl of her lips. The Senior Surgeon's self-confessed blush lent speed to her tongue. "I think I might be privileged to ask what it was for. You see, I presented the flowers to the board meeting. Was it for self-sacrifice?" Her eyes challenged his.

"You are capable of talking more nonsense and being more impertinent than any nurse I have ever known. May I pass?" His eyes returned her challenge, blazing.

But she never moved; the mind-string once broken, there seemed to be no limit to the thoughts that could come tumbling off the end of her tongue. Her eyes went back to the flower in his coat.

"Perhaps you would like to know that I bought those this morning because they seemed the very breath of spring itself—a bit of promise and gladness. I thought they would keep the day going right."

"Well, they have—for me." And the Senior Surgeon could not resist a look of triumph.

"The trustees"—she drew in a quick breath and put out a steadying hand on the banisters—"you mean—they have given up the incurable ward?"

He nodded. His voice took on a more genial tone. He felt he could generously afford to be pleasant and patient toward the one who had not succeeded. "It was something that was bound to happen sooner or later. Can't you see that yourself? But I am sorry, very sorry for you."

Suddenly, and for the first time in their long sojourn together in Saint Margaret's, he became wholly conscious of the girl before him. He realized that Margaret MacLean had grown into a vital and vitalizing personality—a force with which those who came in contact would have to reckon. She stood before him now, frozen into a gray, accusing figure.

"Are you ill?" he found himself asking.

"No."

He shifted his weight uneasily to the other foot. "Is there anything you want?"

Her face softened into the little-girl look. Her eyes brimmed with a sadness past remedy. "What a funny question from you—you, who have taken from me the only thing I ever let myself want—the love and dependence of those children. Success, and having whatever you want, are such common things with you, that you must count them very cheap; but you can't judge what they mean to others—or what they may cost them."

"As I said before, I am sorry, very sorry you have lost your position here; but you have no one but yourself to blame for that. I should have been very glad to have you remain in the new surgical ward; you are one of the best operative nurses I ever had." He added this in all justice to her; and to mitigate, if he could, his own feeling of discomfort.

Margaret MacLean smiled grimly. "Thank you. I was not referring to the loss of my position, however; that matters very little."

"It should matter." The voice of the Senior Surgeon became instantly professional. "Every nurse should put her work, satisfactorily and scientifically executed, before everything else. That is where you are radically weak. Let me remind you that it is your sole business to look after the physical betterment of your patients—nothing else; and the sooner you give up all this sentimental, fanciful nonsense the sooner you will succeed."

"You are wrong. I should never succeed that way—never. Some cases may need only the bodily care—maybe; but you are a very poor doctor, after all, if you think that is all that children need—or half the grown-ups. There are more people ailing with mind-sickness and heart-sickness, as well as body-sickness, than the world would guess, and you've just got to nurse the whole of them. You will succeed, whether you ever find this out or not; but you will miss a great deal out of your life."

Anger was rekindling in the eyes of the Senior Surgeon; and Margaret MacLean, seeing, grew gentle—all in a minute.

"Oh, I wish I could make you understand. You have always been so strong and well and sufficient unto yourself, it's hard, I suppose, to be able to think or see life through the iron slats of a hospital crib. Just make believe you had been a little crippled boy, with nothing belonging to you, nothing back of you to remember, nothing happy coming to you but what the nurses or the doctors or the trustees thought to bring. And then make believe you were cured and grew up. Wouldn't you remember what life had been in that hospital crib, and wouldn't you fight to make it happier for the children coming after you? Why, the incurable ward was my whole life—home, family, friends, work; everything wrapped up in nine little crippled bodies. It was all I asked or expected of life. Oh, I can tell you that a foundling, with questionable ancestry, with no birth-record or blood-inheritance to boast of, claims very little of the every-day happiness that comes to other people. And yet I was so glad to be alive—and strong and needed by those children that I could have been content all my life with just that."

The Senior Surgeon cleared his throat, preparatory to making some comment, but the nurse raised a silencing finger.

"Wait! there is one thing more. What you have taken from me is the smallest part. The children pay double—treble as much. I pay only with my heart and faith; they pay with their whole lives. Remember that when you install your new surgical ward—and don't reckon it too cheap."

She left him still clearing his throat; and when she came out of the board-room a few seconds later with the green Devonshire bowl in her arms he had disappeared.

Margaret MacLean found Ward C as she had left it. As she was putting down the primroses, on the table in the center of the room she caught Bridget's white face beckoning to her eagerly. Softly she went over to her cot.

"What is it, dear?"

"Miss Peggie darlin', if ye'd only give me leave to talk quiet I'd have the childher cheered up in no time."

"Would you promise not to make any noise?"

"Promise on m' heart! I'll have 'em all asleep quicker 'n nothin'. Ye see, just."

"Very well. I'll be back after supper to see if the promise has been kept." She stooped, brushed away the curls, and kissed the little white forehead. "Oh, Bridget! Bridget! no matter what happens, always remember to keep happy!"

"Sure an' I will," agreed Bridget; and she watched the nurse go out, much puzzled.

VI
THE PRIMROSE RING

Bridget, oldest of the ward, general caretaker and best beloved, hunched herself up on her pillows until she was sitting reasonably straight, and clapped her hands. "Whist!" she called, softly. "Whist there, all o' ye! What's ailin'?"

Eight woebegone pairs of eyes turned in her direction.

"Ye needn't be afeared o' speakin'. Miss Peggie give us leave to talk quiet."

"It's them trusters," wailed Peter. "They come a-peekin' round to see we don't get well."

"They alters calls us 'uncurables,'" moaned Susan.

"Pig of water-drinking Americans!" came from the last cot.

"Ye shut up, Michael! Who did ye ever hear say that?"

"Mine fader." And Michael spat in a perfect imitation thereof.

"Well, don't ye ever say it ag'in—do ye hear? Miss Peggie's American, and so's the House Surgeon, an' it's the next best thing to bein' Irish—which every one can't be, the Lord knows. Now them trusters is heathen, an' they don't know nothin' more'n heathen, an' we ought to be easy on 'em for bein' so ignorant."

"They ken us 'll nae mair be gettin' weel," said Sandy, mournfully.

"Aw, ye're talkin' foolish entirely. What do ye think that C on the door means?"

A silence, significant of much brain-racking, followed.

"C stands for children," announced Susan, triumphantly.

"Aye, it does that, but there be's somethin' more."

"Crutches," suggested Pancho, tentatively.

"Aw, go on wid ye," laughed Bridget. "Ye're 'way off." She paused a moment impressively. "C means 'cured.' '*Childher Cured*,' that's what! Now all we've got to do is to forget trusters an' humps an' pains an' them disagreeable things, an' think o' somethin' pleasant."

"Ain't nothin' pleasant ter think of in er horspital," wailed John, the present disheartenment clouding over all past happiness.

"Ain't, neither," agreed James.

"Aye, there be," contradicted Sandy. "Dinna ye ken the wee gray woman 'at cam creepity round an' smiled?"

"She was nice," said Susan, with obvious approval. "Do ye think, now, she might ha' been me aunt?"

A chorus of positive negation settled all further speculation, while Bridget bluntly inquired. "Honest to goodness, Susan, do ye think the likes o' ye could belong to the likes o' that?"

Pancho broke the painful silence by reverting to the original topic in hand. "Mi' Peggie pleasant too," he suggested, smiling adorably.

"But we've not got either of 'em no longer, so they're no good now," Peter unfortunately reminded every one.

"Don't ye know there be's always somethin' pleasant to think about if ye just hunt round a bit, an' things an' feelin's never get that bad ye can't squeeze out some pleasantment. Don't ye mind the time the trusters had planned to give us all paint-boxes for Christmas, an' half of us not able to hold a brush, let alone paint things, an' Miss Peggie blarneyed them round into givin' us books? Don't ye mind? Now we've got somethin' pleasant here, right now—" And Bridget smiled.

"What?"

"May Eve."

"What's that?"

"'Tain't nothin'," said Susan, sliding back disappointedly on her pillow.

"Sure an' it is," said Bridget; "it's somethin' grand."

"'Tain't nothin'," persisted Susan, "but a May party in Cen'ral Park. Every one takes somethin' ter eat in a box, an' the boys play ball an' the girls dance round, an' the cops let you run on the grass. I knows all about it, fer my sister Katie was 'queen' onct."

"We couldn't play ball, ner run on the grass, ner anything," said Peter, regretfully.

"'Tisn't what Susan says at all," said Bridget, by way of consolation. "If ye'll harken to me a minute, just, I'll be afther tellin' ye what it is."

Ward C became instantly silent—hopefully expectant; Bridget had led them into pleasant places too often for them not to believe in her implicitly and do what she said.

"May Eve," began Bridget, slowly, "is the night o' the year when the faeries come throopin' out o' the ground to fly about on twigs o' thorn an' dance to the music o' the faery pipers. They're all dthressed in wee green jackets an' caps, an' 'tis grand luck to any that sees them. And all the wishes good childher make on May Eve are sure to come thrue." She stopped a moment. "Let's make believe; let's make believe—" Her eyes fell on the primroses, and for the first time she recognized them. "Holy Saint Bridget! them's faery primroses!"

Ward C was properly impressed. Eight little figures sat up as straight as they could; eight pairs of eager eyes followed Bridget's pointing finger and gazed in speechless wonder at the green Devonshire bowl.

"Do ye think, Sandy, that ye could scrooch out o' bed an' hump yerself over to them? If Pether tries he's sure to tumble over, an' some one might hear."

Sandy looked at the flowers without enthusiasm. "Phat are ye wantin' wi' 'em?"

"I'll tell ye when ye get there. Just thry; ye'll be yondther afore ye know it."

Cautiously Sandy rolled over on his stomach and pushed two shrunken little legs out from the covers. Putting them gingerly to the floor, he stood up, holding fast to the bed; then working his way from bed to bed, he reached the table at last, spurred on by Bridget's irresistible blarney:

"Sure ye're walkin' grand, Sandy. I never saw any one puttin' one leg past another smarther than what ye are. Ye'd fetch up to Aberdeen i' no time if ye kept on at the pace ye are goin'."

Pride lies above pain; and Sandy held his head very high as he steadied himself by the table and looked toward Bridget for further orders.

[Illustration: Sandy held his head very high as he steadied himself by the table and looked toward Bridget for further orders.]

"Phat wull a do the noo?" he asked.

In the excitement Bridget had pulled herself to the foot of the cot; and there, eyes shining and cheeks growing pinker and pinker, she held her breath while the pleasantest thought of all shaped itself somewhere under the shock of red curls.

"Ye could never guess in a hundthred years what I was thinkin' this minute," she burst forth, ecstatically.

Eight mouths opened wide in anticipated wonder; but no one thought of guessing.

"I'm thinkin'—I'm thinkin' we could make a primrose ring the night. Is there any knowledgeable one among ye that knows aught of a primrose ring?"

Eight heads shook an emphatic negative.

"Aye, wasn't I sayin' so! Well, sure, a primrose ring is a faery ring; an' any one that makes it an' steps inside, wishin' a wish, is like to have anythin' at all happen them afore they steps out of it ag'in."

Eight breaths were drawn in and sighed out with the shivering delight that always accompanies that feeling which lies between fear and desire; likewise, eight delicious thrills zigzagged up eight cold little spines. Then Bridget shook a commanding finger at Sandy.

"Ye take them flowers out o' the pot an' dthrop them, one by one, till ye have the ground covered from the head of Pancho's bed to the tail o' Michael's. 'Twon't make the whole of a ring, but if ye crook it out i' the middle to the wall yondther, 'twill be like enough."

With a doubtful eye Sandy spanned the distance. "Na—na. Gien a hustled a wud be a dee'd loonie afore a had 'em spilled."

"Aw, go on!" chorused the watchers.

"Thry, just," urged Bridget, "an' we'll sing 'Onward, Christian Soldier' to hearten ye up."

Eight shrill voices piped out the tune; and Sandy, caught by its martial spirit, before he knew it was limping a circle about the beds, marking his trail with golden blossoms. Luckily for Ward C, the nurse on duty during the dinner-hour was in the medical ward, with the door closed. And when she came back to her listening post in the corridor the last word had been sung, the last flower dropped, and Sandy was in his cot again, stretching tired little legs under the covers.

Perhaps the geometrician, or the accurate-minded reader, will doubt whether the primrose ring was made at all—seeing that the wall of Ward C cut off nearly thirty degrees of it. But in the world of fancy geometrical accuracy does not hold; and the only important thing is believing that the ring has been made. I have known of a few who could step inside the faery circle whenever they willed, and without a visible primrose about; but for most of us the blossoms are needed to make the enchantment.

This is one of the heritages that come to those who are lucky enough to dwell much in the world of fancy. They can wish for things and possess them, and enjoy them without actually grasping them with their two hands and saying, "These are my personal belongings." Material things are rather a nuisance, on the whole, for they have to be dusted and kept in order, repatched or repainted; and if one wishes to carry them about there are always the bother of packing and the danger of losing. But these other possessions are different—they are with us wherever we go and whenever we want them—to-day, to-morrow, or for eternity.

"If we had the wee red wishin'-cap," said Bridget, thoughtfully, "we'd not have to be waitin' for what's likely to happen. We could just wish ourselves into Tir-na-n'Og."

"What's that?" demanded Peter.

"'Tis the place the faeries live in, an' 'tis in Irelan'. Sure, 'tis easy gettin' the cap," continued Bridget, with conviction. "All ye need do is to say afther me, 'I wish—I wish for the wee red cap,' an' ye have it."

Bridget extended her hands, palms upward, and the others followed her example; and together they whispered: "I wish—I wish for the wee red cap."

Immediately Bridget's hands closed over a cubic inch of atmosphere, and she cried, exultantly, "Hold on to it tight an' slip it on your head quick—afore it gets from ye!"

Only seven pairs of hands obeyed—Michael protested.

"I have nothinks got," he said, disgustedly.

"Shut up!" And Bridget shook a menacing fist at him. "He's foolish entirely. He thinks he hasn't anythin' foreby he can't see it. Now, all together, 'We wish—'"

"Can we go 'thout any clothes?" interrupted Susan. "We'd feel awful queer in nightshirts."

"Don't ye worry, darlin'. Like as not when we get there the queen herself 'll open a monsthrous big chest where they keeps all the faery clothes, an' let us choose anythin' at all we wants to wear."

"Pants?" queried Peter, eagerly.

"Sure, an' silk dresses an' straw hats wi' ribbon on them, an—"

"Will shoes in the chest be?" Pancho was very anxious; he had never had a pair of shoes in all his six years.

Bridget beamed. "Not i' the chest; but I'll be tellin' ye how ye'll come by them. When we get there we'll look about for a blackthorn-bush—an' there—like as not—in undther it—will be a wee man wi' a leather apron across his knee—the leprechaun, big as life!"

"What's him?"

"Faith I'm tellin' ye—'tis the faery cobbler. An' the minute he slaps the tail of his eye on us he'll sing out: 'Hello, Pancho an' Sandy an' Susan an' all o' yez. I've your boots finished, just.' An' wi' that he'll fetch down the nine pairs an' hand them round."

A sigh of blissful contentment started from the cot by the door, burbled down the length of the ward, and vanished out of the window. Is there anything dearer to the pride of a child than boots—new boots?

Bridget took up the dropped thread and went on. "An' afther that the leprechaun reaches for his crock o' gold an' pulls out a penny. Ye can buy anythin' i' the whole world wi' a faery penny."

"Anythinks!" said Michael, skeptically.

"That's what I said."

"Could yer buy a dorg?" Peter asked, opening one renegade eye.

"Sure—a million dogs."

"Don't want a million. Want jus' one real live black dorg—named Toby—wiv yeller spots an' half-legs—an' long ears—an' a stand-up tail—an' legs—an' long—long—long—" The renegade eye closed tight and Peter was smiling at something afar off.

An antiphonal chorus of yawns broke the hush that followed, while Bridget worked herself back under the covers.

"A ken the penny micht be buyin' a hame," came in a drowsy voice from Sandy's crib. "'Twad be a hame in Aberdeen—wi' trees an' flo'ers an' mickle wee creepit things—an'—Miss Peggie—an'—us—"

"Sure, an' it could be buyin' a grand home in Irelan', the same," Bridget beamed; and then she added, struck forcibly with an afterthought: "But what would be the sense of a home anywheres but here—furninst—within easy reach of a crutch or a wheeled chair? Tell me that!"

Sandy grunted ambiguously; and Bridget took up again the thread of her recounting.

"Ye could never be guessin' half o' the sthrange adventures we'll be havin'! Like as not Sandy 'll be gettin' his hump lifted off him. I mind the story—me mother often told it me. There was a humpy back in Irelan', once, who went always about wi' song in his heart an' another on his lips; an' one day he fetched up inside a faery rath. The pipers were pipin' an' the Wee People was dancin', an' while they was dancin' they was singin' like this: 'Monday an' Tuesday—an' Monday an' Tuesday—an' Monday an' Tuesday'—an' it sounded all jerky and bad. 'That's a terrible poor song,' says the humpy, speakin' out plain. 'What's that?' says the faeries, stoppin' their dance an' gatherin' round him. "'Tis mortal poor music ye are making' says the humpy ag'in. 'Can ye improve it any?' asked the faeries. 'I can that,' says the humpy. 'Add Wednesday to it an' ye'll have double as good a song.' An' when the faeries tried it it was so pretty, an' they was so pleased, they took the hump off him."

Sandy had curled up like a kitten; his eyes were shut, and he was smiling, too. Every one was very quiet; only Rosita moved, reaching out a frightened hand to Bridget.

"Fwaid," she lisped. "All dark—fwaid to do."

"Whist, darlin', ye needn't be afeared. Bridget 'll hold tight to your hand all the way. An' the stars will be out there makin' it bright—so bright—foreby the stars are the faeries' old rush-lights. When they're all burned out, just, they throw them up i' the sky—far as ever they can—an' God reaches out an' catches them. Then He sets them all a-burnin' ag'in, so's the wee angel babies can see what road to be takin'. An' Sandy 'll lose his hump—an' Michael 'll get a new heart—maybe—that won't bump—an' they'll put all the trusters in cages—all but the nice Wee One—cages like they have in the circus— An' they'll never get out to pester us—never—never—no—more—" Bridget's voice trailed off into the distance, carrying with it the last of Rosita's fearing consciousness.

Ward C had suddenly become empty—empty except for a row of tumbled beds and nine little tired-out, cast-off bodies. They had been shed as easily as a boy slips out of his dusty, uncomfortable overalls on a late sultry afternoon, and leaves them behind him on a shady bank, while he plunges, head first, into the cool, dark waters of the swimming-pool just below him, which have been calling and calling and calling.

VII
AND BEYOND

What happened beyond the primrose ring is, perhaps, rather a crazy-quilt affair, having to be patched out of the squares and three-cornered bits of Fancy which the children remembered to bring back with them. I have tried to piece them together into a fairly substantial pattern; but, of course, it can be easily ripped out and raveled into nothing. So I beg of you, on the children's account, to handle it gently, for they believe implicitly in the durability of the fabric.

Sandy remembered the beginning of it—the plunge straight across the primrose ring into the River of Make-Believe; and how they paddled over like puppies—one after another. It was perfectly safe to swim, even if you had never swum before; and the only danger was for those who might stop in the middle of the river and say, or think, "A dinna believe i' faeries." Whoever should do this would sink like a stone, going down, down, down until he struck his bed with a thud and woke, crying.

It was starlight in Tir-na-n'Og—just as Bridget had said it would be—only the stars were far bigger and brighter. The children stood on the white, pebbly beach and shook themselves dry; while Bridget showed them how to pull down their nightshirts to keep them from shrinking, and how to wring out their faery caps to keep the wishes from growing musty or mildewed. After that they met the faery ferryman, who—according to Sandy—"wore a wee kiltie o' reeds, an' a tammie made frae a loch-lily pad wi' a cat-o'-nine-tail tossel, lukin' sae ilk the brae ye wad niver ken he was a mon glen ye dinna see his legs, walkin'." He told them how he ferried over all the "old bodies" who had grown feeble-hearted and were too afraid to swim.

It was Pancho who remembered best about the leprechaun—how they found him sitting cross-legged under the blackthorn-bush with a leather apron spread over his knees, and how he had called out—just as Bridget had said he would:

"Hello, Pancho and Susan and Sandy and all!"

"Have you any shoes got?" Pancho shouted.

The faery cobbler nodded and pointed with his awl to the branches above his head; there hung nine pairs of little green shoes, curled at the toes, with silver buckles, all stitched and soled and ready to wear.

"Will they fit?" asked Pancho, breathlessly.

"Faery shoes always fit. Now reach them down and hand them round."

This Pancho did with despatch. Nine pairs of little white feet were thrust joyously into the green shoes and buckled in tight. On looking back, Pancho was quite sure that this was the happiest moment of his life. The children squealed and clapped their hands and cried:

"They fit fine!"

"Shoes is grand to wear!"

"I feel skippy."

"I feel dancy."

Whereupon they all jumped to their feet and with arms wide-spread, hand clasping hand, they ringed about the cobbler and the thorn-bush. They danced until there was not a scrap of breath left in their bodies; then they tumbled over and rolled about like a nest of young puppies, while the cobbler laughed and laughed until he held his sides with the aching.

It was here that everybody remembered about the faery penny; in fact, that was the one thing remembered by all. And this is hardly strange; if you or I ever possessed a faery penny—even in the confines of a primrose ring—we should never forget it.

It was Bridget, however, who reminded the leprechaun. "Ye haven't by any chance forgotten somethin' ye'd like to be rememberin', have ye?" she asked, diplomatically.

"I don't know," and the cobbler pulled his thinking-lock. "What might it be?"

"Sure, it might be a faery penny," and Bridget eyed him anxiously.

The cobbler slapped his apron and laughed again. "To be sure it might—and I came near forgetting it."

He reached, over and pulled up a tuft of sod at his side; for all one could have told, it might have been growing there, neighbor to all the other sods. Underneath was a dark little hole in the ground; and out of this he brought a brown earthen crock.

"The crock o' gold!" everybody whispered, awesomely.

"Aye, the crock o' gold," agreed the cobbler. "But I keep it hidden, for there is naught that can make more throuble—sometimes." He raised the lid and took out a single shining piece. "Will one do ye?"

Nine heads nodded eloquently, while nine hands were stretched out eagerly to take it.

"Bide a bit. Ye can't all be carrying it at the one time. I think ye had best choose a treasurer."

Bridget was elected unanimously. She took the penny and deposited it in the heel of her faery shoe.

"Mind," said the leprechaun as they were turning to go, "ye mind a faery penny will buy but the one thing. See to it that ye are all agreed on the same thing."

The children chorused an assent and skipped merrily away. And here is where Peter's patch joins Pancho's.

They had not gone far over the silvery-green meadow—three shadow-lengths, perhaps—when they saw something coming toward them. It was coming as fast as half-legs could carry it; and it was wagging a *long*, stand-up tail. Everybody guessed in an instant that it was Peter's "black dorg wiv yeller spots."

"Who der thunk it? Who der thunk it?" shouted Peter, jumping up and down; and then he knelt on the grass, his arms flung wide open, while he called: "Toby, Toby! Here's me!"

Of course Toby knew Peter—that goes without saying. He barked and wagged his tail and licked Peter's face; in fact, he did every dog-thing Peter had longed for since Peter's mind had first fashioned him.

"Well," and Bridget put both arms akimbo and smiled a smile of complete satisfaction, "what was I a-tellin' ye, anyways? Faith, don't it beat all how things come thrue—when ye think 'em pleasant an' hard enough?"

Peter remembered the wonderful way their feet skimmed over the ground—"'most like flyin'." Not a blade of grass bent under their weight, not a grain of sand was dislodged; and—more marvelous than all—there was no tiredness, no aching of joint or muscle. All of which was bound to happen when feet were shod with faery shoes.

"See me walk!" cried some one.

"See me run!" cried some one else.

"See me hop and jump!"

And Bridget added, "Faith, 'tis as easy as lyin' in bed."

They were no longer alone; hosts of Little People passed them, going in the same direction. Peter said most of them rode "straddle-legs" on night birds or moths, while some flew along on a funny thing that was horse before and weeds behind. I judge this must have been the buchailin buidhe or benweed, which the faeries bewitch and ride the same as a witch mounts her broomstick.

And everybody who passed always called out in the friendliest way, "Hello, Peter!" or "Hello, Bridget!" or "The luck rise with ye!" which is the most common of all greetings in Tir-na-n'Og.

"Gee!" was Peter's habitual comment after the telling, "maybe it wasn't swell havin' 'em know us—names an' all. Betcher life we wasn't cases to them—no, siree!"

It was Susan who remembered best how everything looked—Susan, who had never been to the country in all her starved little life—that is, if one excepts the times Margaret MacLean had taken her on the Ward C "special." She told so well how all the trees and flowers were fashioned that it was an easy matter putting names to them.

In the center of Tir-na-n'Og towered a great hill; but instead of its being capped with peak or rocks it was gently hollowed at the top, as though in the beginning, when it was thrown up molten from the depths of somewhere, a giant thumb had pressed it down and smoothed it round and even. All about the brim of it grew hawthorns and rowans and hazel-trees. In the grass, everywhere, were thousands and millions of primroses, heart's-ease, and morning-glories; all crowded together, so Susan said, like the patterns on the Persian carpet in the board-room. It was all so beautiful and faeryish and heart-desired that "yer'd have said it wasn't real if yer hadn't ha' knowed it was."

The children stood on the brink of the giant hollow and clapped their hands for the very joy of seeing it all; and there—a little man stepped up to them and doffed his cap. The queen wanted them—she was waiting for them by the throne that very minute; and the little man was to bring them to her.

Now that throne—according to Susan—was nothing like the thrones one finds in stories or Journeys through palaces to see. It was not cold, hard, or forbidding; instead, it was as soft and green and pillowy as an inflated golf-bunker might be, and just high and comfortable enough for the baby faeries to discover it and go to sleep there whenever they felt tired. The throne was full of them when the children looked, and some one was tumbling them off like so many kittens.

"That is the queen," said the little man, pointing.

The children stood on tiptoes and craned their necks the better to see; but it was not until they had come quite close that they saw that her dress was gray, and her hair was gray, and she was small, and her face was like—

"Bless me if it ain't!" shouted Susan in amazement. "It's Sandy's wee creepity woman!"

The queen smiled when she saw them. She reached out her hands and patted theirs in turn, asking, "Now what is your name, dearie?"

"Are ye sure ye're the queen?" gasped Bridget.

"Maybe I am—and maybe I'm not," was the answer.

"Then ye been't the wee gray woman—back yonder?" asked Sandy.

"Maybe I'm not—and maybe I am." And then she laughed. "Dear children, it doesn't matter in the least who I am. I look a hundred different ways to a hundred different people. Now let me see—I think you wanted some—clothes."

A long, rapturous sigh was the only answer. It lasted while the queen got down on her knees—just like an every-day, ordinary person—and pulled from under the throne a great carved chest. She threw open the lid wide; and there, heaped to the top and spilling over, were dresses and mantles and coats and trousers and caps. They were all lengths, sizes, and fashions—just what you most wanted after you had been in bed for years and never worn anything but a hospital shirt; and everything was made of cloth o' dreams and embroidered with pearls from the River of Make-Believe.

"You can choose whatever you like, dearies," said the queen. And that—according to Susan—was the best of all.

Next came the dancing; the Apostles remembered about that co-operatively. They had donned pants of pink and yellow, respectively, with shirts of royal purple and striked stockings, when the pipers began to play. James said it sounded like soldiers marching; John was certain that it was more like a circus; but I am inclined to believe that they played "The Music of Glad Memories" and "What-is-Sure-to-Come-True," for those are the two popular airs in Tir-na-n'Og.

Away and away must have danced pairs of little feet that had never danced before, and pairs of old feet that had long ago forgotten how; and millions of faery feet, for no one can dance half as joyously as when faeries dance with them. And I have heard it said that the pipers there can play sadness into gladness, and tears into laughter, and old age young again; and that those who have ever danced to the music of faery pipes never really grow heavy-hearted again.

Needless to say, the Apostles danced together, and Peter danced with Toby; and it must have been the maddest, merriest dance, for they never told about it afterward without bursting into peal after peal of laughter. Truth to tell, the Apostles' patch of fancy ended right there—all raveling out into smiles and squirms of delight.

Another memory of Sandy's adjoins that of the Apostles'; and he told it with great precision and regard for the truth.

Ever since crossing the River of Make-Believe Sandy had been able to think of nothing but the story Bridget had told—the very last thing in Ward C— and ever since he had left the leprechaun's bush behind he had been wondering and scheming how he could get rid of his hump. He was the only person in Tir-na-n'Og that night who did not dance. Unnoticed, he climbed into a corner of the throne—among the sleeping baby faeries—and there he thought hard. As he listened to the pipers' music he shook his head mournfully.

"A canna make music mair bonny nor that—a canna," he said; and he set about searching through the scraps of his memory for what music he did know. There were the hymns they sang every Sunday at Saint Margaret's; but he somewhat doubted their appropriateness here. Then there were the songs his mother had sung to him home in Aberdeen. Long ago the words had been forgotten; but often and often he had hummed the music of them over to himself when he was going to sleep—it was good music for that. One of the airs popped into his mind that very minute; it was a Jacobite song about "Charlie," and he started to hum it softly. Close on the humming came an idea—a braw one; it made him sit up in the corner of the throne and clap his hands, while his toes wriggled exultantly inside his faery shoes.

"A can do't—a can!" He shouted it so loud that the baby faeries woke up and asked what he was going to do, and gathered about him to listen the better.

The pipers played until there were no more memories left and everything had come true; and the queen came back to her throne to find Sandy waiting, eager-eyed, for her.

"A have a bonny song made for ye. Wull ye tak it frae me noo?"

"Take what?"

"The hump. Ye tuk it frae the ither loonie gien he made ye some guid music; an' a ha' fetched ye mair—here." And he tapped his head to signify that it was not written down.

"Is the song ready, now?"

Sandy nodded.

"Then turn about and sing it loud enough for all to hear; they must be the judges if the song is worth the price of a hump." And the queen smiled very tenderly.

Sandy did as he was bid; he clasped his hands tightly in front of him. "'Tis no for the faeries," he explained. "Ye see—they be hardly needin' ony music, wi' muckle o' their ain. 'Tis for the children—the children i' horspitals—a bonny song for them to sleepit on." He marked the rhythm a moment with his foot, and hummed it through once to be sure he had it. Then he broke out clearly into the old Jacobite air—with words of his own making:

> "Ye weave a bonny primrose ring;
>   Ye hear the River callin';
> Ye ken the Land whaur faeries sing—
>   Whaur starlicht beams are fallin'.
> 'Tis there the pipers play things true;
>   'Tis there ye'll gae—my dearie—
> The bonny Land 'at waits for you,
>   Whaur ye'll be nae mair weary.
>
> "A wee man by a blackthorn-tree
>   Maun stitchit shoes for dancin',
> An' there's a pair for ye an' me—
>   To set our feet a-prancin'.
> 'Tis muckle gladness 'at ye'll find
>   In Tir-na-n'Og, my dearie;
> The bonny Land 'at's aye sae kind,
>   Whaur ye'll be nae mair weary.
>
> "Ye'll ken the birdeen's blithie song,
>   Ye'll hark till flo'ers lauchen;
> An' see the faeries trippit long
>   By brook an' brae an' bracken.
> Sae doon your heid—an' shut your een;
>   Gien ye'd be away, my dearie—
> An' the bonny sauncy faery queen
>   Wull keep ye—nae mair weary."

You may think it uncommonly strange that Sandy could make a song like this, by himself; but, you see, he was not entirely alone—there were the baby faeries. They helped a lot; as fast as ever he thought out the words they rhymed them for him—this being a part of the A B C of faery education.

When the song was finished Sandy turned to the queen again.
"Aighe—wull it do?"

"If the faeries like it, and think it good enough to send down to the children, they will have it all learned by heart and will sing it back to you in a minute. Listen! Can you hear anything?"

For a moment only the rustle of the trees could be heard. Sandy strained his ears until he caught a low, sobbing sound coming through the hazel-leaves.

"'Tis but the wind—greetin'," he said, wistfully.

"Listen again!"

The sound grew, breaking into a cadence and a counter-cadence, and thence into a harmony. "'Tis verra ilk the grand pipe-organ i' the kirk, hame in Aberdeen."

"Listen again!"

Mellow and sweet came the notes of the Jacobite air—a bar of it; and then the faeries began to sing, sending the song back to Sandy like a belated echo:

"Ye weave a bonny primrose ring;
　Ye hear the River callin';
Ye ken the Land whaur faeries sing—
　Whaur starlicht beams are fallin'."

"For the love o' Mike!" laughed Sandy. "A'm unco glad—a am." He dropped to his knees beside the queen and nestled his cheek in the hand that was resting in her lap. "'Tis aricht noo." And he sighed contentedly.

And it was. The queen leaned over and lifted off the hump as easily as you might take the cover from a box. Sandy stretched himself and yawned—after the fashion of any one who has been sleeping a long time in a cramped position; and without being in the least conscious of it, he sidled up to the arm of the throne and rubbed his back up and down—to test the perfect straightness of it.

"'Tis gone—guid! Wull it nae mair coom back?" And he eyed the queen gravely.

"Never to be burdensome, little lad. Others may think they see it there, but for you the back will be straight and strong."

Rosita came back—empty-handed; she was so busy holding tight to Bridget's hand and getting ready to be afraid that she forgot everything else. As for Michael, he gave his patch into Bridget's keeping; which brings us to what Bridget remembered.

From the moment that the penny had been given over to her she had been weighed down with a mighty responsibility. The financier of any large syndicate is bound to feel harassed at times over the outcome of his investments; and Bridget felt personally accountable for the forthcoming happiness due the eight other stockholders in her company. She was also mindful of what had happened in the past to other persons who had speculated heedlessly or unwisely with faery gifts. There was the case of the fisherman and his wife, and the aged couple and their sausage, and the old soldier; on the other hand, there was the man from Letterkenny who had hoarded his gold and had it turn to dry leaves as a punishment. She must neither keep nor spend foolishly.

"Sure I'll think all round a thing twict afore I have my mind made to anythin'; then I'll keep it made for a good bit afore I give over the penny."

She repeated this advice while she considered all possible investments, but she found nothing to her liking. The children made frequent suggestions, such as bagpipes and clothes-chests, and contrivances for feast-spreading and transportation; and Susan was strongly in favor of a baby faery to take back to Miss Peggie. But to all of these Bridget shook an emphatic negative.

"Sure ye'd be tired o' the lot afore ye'd gone half-way back. Like as not we'll never have another penny to spend as long as we live, an' I'm goin' to see that ye'll all get somethin' that will last."

She was beginning to fear that theirs would be the fate of the man from Letterkenny, when she chanced upon Peter and Toby performing for the benefit of the pipers.

"Them trusters will never be lettin' Pether take that dog back to the horspital," she thought, mindful of the sign in Saint Margaret's yard that dogs were not allowed. "He'd have to be changin' him back into a make-believe dog to get him in at all; an' Pether'd never be satisfied wi' him that way, now—afther havin' him real."

Her trouble took her to the queen. "Is there any way of buyin' a dog into a horspital?" she asked, solemnly.

"I think it would be easier to buy a home to put him in."

"Could ye—could ye get one for the price of a penny?" Bridget considered her own question, and coupled it with something she remembered Sandy had been wishing for back in Ward C. "Wait a minute; I'll ask ye another. Could ye be buyin' a home for childher an' dogs for the price of a penny?"

The queen nodded.

"Would it be big enough for nine childher—an' one dog; an' would it be afther havin' all improvements like Miss Peggie an' the House Surgeon?"

Again the queen nodded.

Bridget lowered her voice. "An' could we put up a sign furninst, 'No Trusters Allowed'?"

"I shouldn't wonder."

"Then," said Bridget, with decision, "I've thought all round it twict an' my mind's been made to stay; we'll buy a home."

She made a hollow of her two hands and called, "Whist—whist there, all o' yez! Pether an' Pancho—Michael—Susan—do ye hear!" And when she had them rounded up, she counted them twice to make sure they were all present. "Now ye listen." Bridget raised a commanding finger to the circle about her while she exhibited the golden penny. "Is there any one objectin' to payin' this down for a home?"

"What kind of a home?" asked Susan, shrewdly.

"Sure the kind ye live in—same as other folks have that don't live in horspitals or asylums."

"Hurrah!" chorused everybody, and Bridget sighed with relief.

"Faith, spendin' money's terrible easy."

She put the penny in the queen's out-stretched hand. "Do I get a piece o' paper sayin' I paid the money on it?" she demanded, remembering her responsibility.

This time the queen shook her head. "No; I give you only my promise; but a promise made across a primrose ring is never broken."

"And Toby?" Peter asked it anxiously.

"You must leave him behind. You see, if you took him back over the River of Make-Believe he would have to turn back into a make-believe dog again; but—I promise he shall be waiting in the home for you."

The queen led them down the hill to the shore again; and there they found the ferry-man ready, waiting. It is customary, I believe, for every one to be ferried home. The river, that way, is treble as wide, and the sandman is always wandering up and down the brink, scattering his sand so that one is apt to get too drowsy to swim the whole distance. The children piled into the boat—all but Michael; he stood clinging fast to the queen's gray dress.

"Don't you want to go back?" she asked, gently.

"Nyet; the heart by me no longer to bump—here," and Michael pointed to the pit of his stomach.

"Aw, come on," called Peter.

But Michael only shook his head and clung closer to the gray dress.

"All right, ferryman; he may stay," said the queen.

"Good-by!" shouted the children. "Don't forget us, Michael."

"Nyet; goo'-by," Michael shouted back; and then he laughed. "You tell Mi' Peggie—I say—Go' blees you!"

And this was Michael's patch.

The ferryman stood in the stem and swung his great oar. Slowly the boat moved, scrunching over the white pebbles, and slipped into the water. The children saw Michael and the queen waving their hands until they had dwindled to shadow-specks in the distance; they watched the wake of starshine lengthen out behind them; they listened to the ripples lapping at the keel. To and fro, to and fro, swayed the ferryman to the swing of his oar. "Sleep—sleep—sleep," sang the river, running with them. Bridget stretched her arms about as many children as she could compass and held them close while eight pairs of eyes slowly—slowly—shut.

VIII
IN WHICH A PART OF THE BOARD HAS DISTURBING DREAMS

It is a far cry from a primrose ring to a disbanded board meeting; but Fancy bridged it in a twinkling and without an effort. She blew the trustees off the door-step of Saint Margaret's, homeward, with an insistent buzzing of "ifs" and "buts" in their ears, and the faint woodsy odor of primroses under their noses.

To each member of the board entering his own home, unsupported by the presence of his fellow-members and the scientific zeal of the Senior Surgeon, the business of the afternoon began to change its aspect. For some unaccountable reason—unless we take Fancy into the reckoning—this sudden abandoning of Ward C did not seem the simple matter of an hour previous; while in perspective even Margaret MacLean's outspokenness became less heinous and more human.

As they settled themselves for the evening, each quietly and alone after his or her particular fashion of comfort, the "ifs" and "buts" were still buzzing riotously; while the primroses, although forgotten, clung persistently to the frills or coat lapels where the Youngest and Prettiest Trustee had put them. There it was that Fancy slipped unnoticed over the threshold of library, den, and boudoir in turn; and with a glint of mischief in her eyes she set the stage in each place to her own liking, while she summoned whatever players she chose to do her bidding.

Now the trustees were very different from the children in the matter of telling what they remembered of that May Eve. Of course they were hampered with all the self-consciousness and skepticism of grown-ups, which would make them quite unwilling to own up to anything strange or out of the conventional path, not in a hundred years. Therefore I am forced to leave their part of the telling to Fancy, and you may believe or discredit as much or as little as you choose; only I am hoping that by this time you have acquired at least a sprinkling of fern-seed in your eyes. You may have forgotten that fern-seed is the most subtle of eye-openers known to Fancy; and that it enables you to see the things that have existed only in your imagination. It is very scarce nowadays, and hard to find, for the bird-fanciers no longer keep it—and the nursery-gardeners have forgotten how to grow it. In the light of what happened afterward, I think you will agree that Fancy has not been far wrong concerning the trustees; she has a way of putting things a little differently, that is all.

To be sure, you may argue that it was all chance, conscience, or even indigestion; because the trustees dined late they must have dined heavily. But if you do, you know very well that Fancy will answer: "Poof! Nothing of the kind. It was a simple matter of primrose magic and—faeries; nothing else." And she ought to know, for she was there.

The President began it.

He sat in his den, yawning over the annual report of the United Charities; he had already yawned a score of times, and the type had commenced running together in a zigzagging line that baffled deciphering. The President inserted a finger in the report to mark his place, making a mental note to consult his oculist the following day; after which he leaned back and closed his eyes for the space of a moment—to clear his vision.

When he opened his eyes again his vision had cleared to such an extent that he was quite positive he was seeing things that were not in the room. Little shadowy figures haunted the dark places: corners, and curtained recesses, and the unlighted hall beyond. They peered at him shyly, with such witching, happy faces and eyes that laughed coaxingly. The President found himself peering back at them and scrutinizing the faces closely. Oddly enough he could recognize many, not by name, of course, but he could place them in the many institutions over which he presided. It was very evident that they were expecting something of him; they were looking at him that way. For once in his life he was at loss for the correct thing to say. He tried closing his eyes two or three times to see if he could not blink them into vanishing; but when he looked again there they were, more eager-eyed than before.

"Well," he found himself saying at last—"well, what is it?"

That was all; but it brought the children like a Hamlin troop to the piper's cry—flocking about him unafraid. Never in all his charitable life had he ever had children gather about him and look up at him this way. Little groping hands pulled at his cuffs or steadied themselves on his knee; more venturesome ones slipped into his or hunted their way into his coat pockets. They were such warm, friendly, trusting little hands—and the faces; the President of Saint Margaret's Free Hospital for Children caught himself wondering why in all his charitable experience he had never had a child overstep a respectful distance before, or look at him save with a strange, alien expression.

He sat very still for fear of frightening them off; he liked the warmth and friendliness of their little bodies pressed close to him; there was something pleasantly hypnotic in the feeling of small hands tugging at him. Suddenly he became conscious of a change in the children's faces; the gladness was fading out and in its place was creeping a perplexed, questioning sorrow.

"Don't." And the President patted assuringly as many little backs as he could reach. "What—what was it you expected?"

He was answered by a quivering of lips and more insistent tugs at his pockets. It flashed upon him—out of some dim memory—that children liked surprises discovered unexpectedly in some one's pockets. Was this why they had searched him out? He found himself frantically wishing that he had something stowed away somewhere for them. His hands followed theirs into all the numerous pockets he possessed; trousers, coat, and vest were searched twice over; they were even turned inside out in the last hope of disclosing just one surprise.

"I should think," said the President, addressing himself, "that a man might keep something pleasant in empty pockets. What are pockets for, anyway?"

The children shook their heads sorrowfully.

"Wouldn't to-morrow do?" he suggested, hopefully; but there was no response from the children, and the weight that had been settling down upon him, in the region of his chest, noticeably increased. He tried to shake it off, it was so depressing—like the accruing misfortune of some pending event.

"Don't shake," said a voice behind him; "that isn't your misfortune. You will only shake it off on the children, and it's time enough for them to bear it when they wake up in the morning and find out—"

"Find out what?" The President asked it fearfully.

"Find out—find out—" droned the voice, monotonously.

The President sat up very straight in his chair. "The children—the children." He remembered now—they were the children from the incurable ward at Saint Margaret's.

He sank back with a feeling of great helplessness, and closed his eyes again. And there he sat, immovable, his finger still marking his place in the report of the United Charities.

The Oldest Trustee sat alone, knitting comforters for the Preventorium patients. Like many another elderly person, her usual retiring hour was later than that of the younger members of her household, undoubtedly due to the frequent cat-naps snatched from the evening.

The Oldest Trustee had a habit of knitting the day's events in with her yarn. What she had done and said and heard were all thought over again to the rhythmic click of her needles. And the results at the end of the evening were usually a finished comforter and a comfortable feeling. This night, however, the knitting lagged and the thoughts were unaccountably dissatisfying; she could not even settle down to a cat-nap with the habitual serenity.

"I don't know why I should feel disturbed," and the Oldest Trustee prodded her yarn ball with a disquieting needle, "but I certainly miss the usual gratification of a day well spent."

She closed her eyes, hoping thereby to lose herself for the space of a moment, but instead— She was startled to hear voices at her very elbow; a number of persons must have entered the room, but how they could have done so without her knowing it she could not understand. Of course they thought her asleep; it was just as well to let them think so. She really felt too tired to talk.

"Mother's undoubtedly growing old. Have you noticed how much she naps in the evening, now?" It was the voice of her youngest daughter.

"I heard her telling some one the other day she was five years younger than she is. That's a sure sign," and her son laughed an amused little chuckle.

"I can tell you a surer one." This time it was her oldest daughter—her first-born. "Haven't you noticed how all mother's little peculiarities are growing on her? She is getting so much more dictatorial and preachy. Of course, we know that mother means to be kind and helpful, but she has always been so—tactless—and blunt; and it's growing worse and worse."

"I have often wondered how all her charity people take her; it must come tough on them, sometimes. Gee! Can't you see her raising those lorgnettes of hers and saying, 'My good boy, do you read your Bible?' or, 'My little girl, I hope you remember to be grateful for all you receive.' Say, wouldn't you hate to have charity stuffed down your throat that way?" and the oldest and favorite grandson groaned out his feelings.

"That isn't what I should mind the most." It was the youngest daughter speaking again. "I've been with mother when she has made remarks about the patients in the hospital, loud enough for them to hear, and I was so mortified I wanted to sink through the floor, And you simply can't shut mother up. Of course she doesn't realize how it sounds; she doesn't believe they hear her, but I know they do. I wonder how mother would like to have us stand around her—and we know her and love her—and have us say she was getting deaf, or her hair was coming out, or her memory was beginning to fail, or—"

The Oldest Trustee smiled grimly. "Oh, don't stop, my dear. If there is any other failing you can think of—" She opened her eyes with a start. "Goodness gracious!" she exclaimed. "My grandson is in college five hundred miles away, and my daughter is abroad. Have I been dreaming?"

The Meanest Trustee unlocked the drawer of his desk and took out a cigar. He did not intend that his sons or his servants should smoke at his expense; furthermore, it was well not to spread temptation before others. He took up the evening paper and examined the creases carefully. He wished to make sure it had not been unfolded before; being the one to pay for the news in his house, he preferred to be the first one to read it. The creases proved perfectly satisfactory; so he lighted his cigar, crossed his feet, and settled himself—content in his own comfort. The smoke spun into spirals about his head; and after he had skimmed the cream of the day's events he read more leisurely, stopping to watch the spirals with a certain lazy enjoyment. They seemed to grow increasingly larger. They spun themselves about into all kinds of shapes, wavering and illusive, that defied the somewhat atrophied imagination of the Meanest Trustee.

"Hallucinations," he barked to himself. "I believe I understand now what is implied when people are said to have them."

Suddenly the spirals commenced to lengthen downward instead of upward. To the amazement of the Meanest Trustee he discovered them shifting into human shapes: here was the form of a child, here a youth, here a lover and his lass, here a little old dame, and scores more; while into the corners of the room drifted others that turned into the drollest of droll pipers—with kilt and brata and cap. It made him feel as if he had been dropped into the center of a giant kaleidoscope, with thousands of pieces of gray smoke turning, at the twist of a hand, into form and color, motion and music. The pipers piped; the figures danced, whirling and whirling about him, and their laughter could be heard above the pipers' music.

"Stop!" barked the Meanest Trustee at last; but they only danced the faster. "Stop!" And he shook his fist at the pipers, who played louder and merrier. "Stop!" And he pounded the arms of his chair with both hands. "I hate music! I hate children! I hate noise and confusion! Stop! I say."

Still the pipers played and the figures danced on; and the Meanest Trustee was compelled to hear and see. To him it seemed an interminable time. He would have stopped his ears with his fingers and shut his eyes, only, strangely enough, he could not. But at last it all came to an end—the figures floated laughing away, and the pipers came and stood about him, their caps in their hands out-stretched before him.

He eyed them suspiciously. "What's that for?"

"It is time to pay the pipers," said one.

"Let those who dance pay; that's according to the adage," and he smiled caustically at his own wit.

"It's a false adage," said a second, "like many another that you follow in your world. It is not the ones who dance that should pay, but the ones who keep others from dancing—the ones who help to rob the world of some of its joy. And the ones who rob the most must pay the heaviest. Come!" And he shook his cap significantly.

A sudden feeling of helplessness overpowered the Meanest Trustee. Muttering something about "pickpockets" and "hold-ups," he ferreted around in his pocket and brought out a single coin, which he dropped ungraciously into the insistent cap.

"What's that?" asked the head piper, curiously.

"It looks to me like money—good money—and I'm throwing it away on a parcel of rascals."

"Come, come, my good man," and the piper tapped him gently on the shoulder, in the fashion of a professional philanthropist when he remonstrates with a professional vagrant; "don't you see you are not giving your soul any room to grow in? A great deal of joy might have reached the world across your open palm. Instead, you have crushed it in a hard, tight fist. You must pay now for all the souls you've kept from dancing. Come—fill all our caps."

"Fill!" There was something akin to actual terror in the voice of the Meanest Trustee. He could feel himself growing pale; his tongue seemed to drop back in his throat, choking him. "That would take a great deal of money," he managed to wheeze out at last; and then he braced himself, his hands clutched deep in his pockets. "I will never pay; never, never, never!"

"Oh yes, you will!" and the piper's smile was insultingly cheerful. "It was a great deal of joy, you know," he reminded him. "Come, lads"—to the other pipers—"hold out your caps, there."

The Meanest Trustee had the strange experience of feeling himself worked by a force outside of his own will; it was as if he had been a marionette with a master-hand pulling the wires. Quite mechanically he found himself taking something out of his pocket and dropping it into the caps thrust under his very nose, and at the same time his pockets began to fill with money—his money. In and out, in and out, his hands flew like wooden members, until there was not a coin left and the last piper turned away satisfied. He closed his eyes, for he was feeling very weak; then he became conscious of the touch of a warm, friendly hand on his wrist and he heard the voice of the old family doctor—the one who had set his leg when he was a little shaver and had fallen off the banisters, sliding downstairs.

"You will recover," it was saying. "A good rest is all you need. Sometimes there is nothing so beneficial and speedy as the old-fashioned treatment of bleeding a patient."

Some warm ashes dropped across the wrist of the Meanest Trustee and scattered on the floor; his cigar had gone out.

The Executive Trustee dozed at his study table. For months he had been working his brain overtime; he had still more to demand of it, and he was deliberately detaching it from immediate executive consciousness for a few minutes that he might set it to work again all the harder.

The Executive Trustee knew that he was dozing; but for all that it was unbearable—this feeling of being bound by coil after coil of rope until he could not stir a finger. A terrifying numbness began to creep over him—as if his body had died. The thought came to him like a shock that he had an active, commanding intelligence, still alive, and nothing for it to command. What did people do who had to live with dead, paralyzed bodies, dependent upon others to execute the dictates of their brains? Did not their brains go in the end, too, and leave just a breathing husk behind? The thought became a horror to him.

And yet people did live, just so. Yes, even children. Somewhere—somewhere—he knew of hundreds of them—or were there only a few? He tried to remember, but he could not. He did remember, however, that he had once heard them laughing; and he found himself wondering now at the strangeness of it. He hoped there was some one who would always keep them laughing—they deserved that much out of life, anyway; and some one who could understand and could administer to them lovingly—yes, that was the word—lovingly! As for himself, there was no one who could supply for him that strength and power for action that he had always worshiped; he must exist for the rest of his life simply as a thinking, ineffective intelligence. The Executive Trustee forgot that he was dozing. He wrestled with the ropes that bound him like a crazed man; he called for help again and again, until his lips could make no sound. For the first time in his remembrance he tasted the bitterness of despair. Then it was that the door opened noiselessly and Margaret MacLean entered, her finger to her lips. Coil after coil she unwound until he was free once more and could feel the marvelous response of muscle and nerve impulse. With a cry—half sob, half thankfulness—he flung his arms across the table and buried his face in them.

The Executive Trustee slept heavily, after the fashion of a man exhausted from hard labor.

In the house left by the Richest Trustee a little gray wisp of a woman sat huddled in a great carved chair close to the hearth, thinking and thinking and thinking. The fire was blazing high, trying its best to burn away the heart-cold and loneliness that clung about everything like a Dover fog. For years she had ceased to exist apart from her husband—her thoughts, her wishes, her interests were of his creating; she had drawn her very nourishment of life from his strong, dominant, genial personality. It was parasitic—oh yes, but it had been something rarely beautiful to them both—her great need of him. The need had grown all the greater because no children had come to fill her life; and the need of something to take care of had grown with him. Their love, and her dependence, had become the greatest factors in his life; in hers they were the only ones. Therefore, it was hardly strange, now that he had died, that she should find it hard to take up an individual existence again; to be truthful, she had found it impossible—she had not even existed.

The habit of individual, separate thinking had grown rusty, and as she sat before the hearth ideas came slowly. The room was dim—lighted only by the firelight; and in that dimness her mind began to stir and stretch and yawn itself awake, like a creature that had been hibernating through a long, dark winter. Suddenly the widow of the Richest Trustee broke out into a feeble little laugh—a convalescing laugh that acted as if it was just getting about for the first time.

"I haven't the least idea what is the matter with me," she said, addressing the fire, "but I think—I think—I'm becoming alive again."

The fire gave an appreciative chuckle—it even slapped one of the logs on the back; then it sputtered and blazed the harder, just as if it were ashamed of showing any emotion.

"It is funny," agreed the little gray wisp of a woman, "but I actually feel as I used to when I was a little girl and Christmas Eve had come, or Hallowe'en, and—and— What other night in the year was it that I used to feel creepy and expectant—as if something wonderful was going to happen?"

The fire coughed twice, as if it would have liked to remind her that it was May Eve, but felt it might be an intrusion.

"I believe," she continued, speculatively—"I believe I am going to begin to think things and do them again; and what's more, I believe I am going to like doing them."

The fire chuckled again, and danced about for a minute in an absurd fashion; it was so absurd that one of the logs broke a sap-vessel. After that the fire settled down to its intended vocation, that of making dream-pictures out of red and gold flames, and black, charred embers.

The widow of the Richest Trustee watched them happily for a long time, until they became very definite and actual pictures. Then she got up, went to her desk, and wrote two letters.

The first was addressed to "The Board of Trustees of Saint Margaret's Free Hospital for Children"; the second was addressed to "Miss Margaret MacLean." They were both sealed and mailed that night.

What befell the other trustees does not matter, either from the standpoint of Fancy or of what happened afterward; moreover, it was nearly midnight, and what occurs after that on May Eve does not count.

IX
THE LOVE-TALKER

All through the evening Saint Margaret's had been frankly miserable. Nurses gathered in groups in the nurses' annex and talked about the closing of the incurable ward and the going of Margaret MacLean. The passing of the incurables mattered little to them, one way or another, but they knew what it mattered to the nurse in charge, and they were just beginning to realize what she had meant to them all. The Superintendent felt so much concerned that she dropped her official manner when she chanced upon Margaret MacLean on her way from supper.

"Oh, my dear—my dear"—and the Superintendent's voice had almost broken—"what shall we do without you? You have kept Saint Margaret's human—and wholesome for the rest of us."

The House Surgeon had been miserable unto the third degree. It had forced him into doing all those things he had left undone for months passed; and he bustled through the building—from pharmacy to laboratory and from operating-room to supply-closets—giving the impression of a very scientific man, while he was inwardly praying for a half-dozen minutes alone with Margaret MacLean. He had passed her more than once in the corridors, but she had eluded him each time, brushing by him with a tightening of the lips and a little shake of the head, half pleading, half commanding. At last, in grim despair, he gave up appearances and patrolled the second-floor hall until the night nurse fixed upon him such a greenly suspicious eye that he fled to his quarters—vowing unspeakable things.

Even old Cassie, the scrub-woman, shared in the general misery—Cassie, who had brewed the egg-shell charm against Trustee Days. She had stayed past her hours for a glimpse of "Miss Peggie," with the best intention in the world of cheering her up. When the glimpse came, however, she stood mute—tears channeling the old wrinkled face—while the nurse patted her hands and made her laugh through the tears. In fact, Margaret MacLean had been kept so busy doling out cheer and consolation to others that she had had no time to remember her own trouble—not until Saint Margaret's had gone to bed.

She was on her way for a final visit to her ward—the visit she had told Bridget she would make to see if the promise had been kept—when a line from Hauptman's faery play flashed through her mind: "At dawn we are kings; at night we are only beggars."

How true it was of her—this day. How beggared she felt! The fact that she was very nearly penniless troubled her very little; it was the homelessness—friendlessness—that frightened her. She had never had but two friends: the one who had gone so long ago was past helping her now; the other—

No; she had made up her mind some hours before that she should slip away in the morning without saying anything to the House Surgeon. It would make it so much easier for him. Otherwise—he might—because of his friendship—say or do something he would have to regret all his life. She had been very much in earnest when she had told the Senior Surgeon on the stairs that such as she laid no claim to the every-day happiness that felt to the lot of others. That was why she had kept persistently out of the House Surgeon's way all the evening.

She pushed back the door of Ward C. The night light in the hall outside was shaded; only a glimmer came through the windows from the street lamps below; consequently things could not be seen very clearly or distinguishably in the room. Across the threshold her foot slid over something soft and slippery; stooping, her hand closed upon a flower, while she brushed another. Puzzled, she felt her way over to the table in the center of the room, where she had put the green Devonshire bowl. It was empty.

"That's funny," she murmured, her mind attempting to ferret out an explanation. She dropped to her knees and scanned the floor closely. There they were, the primroses, a curving trail of them stretching from the head of Pancho's bed to the foot of Michael's. She choked back an exclamation just as a shadow cut off the light from the hall. It was a man's shadow, and the voice of the House Surgeon came over the threshold in a whisper:

"What are you doing—burying ghosts?"

"Come and see, and let the light in after you."

The House Surgeon came and stood behind her where she knelt. She looked so little and childlike there that he wanted to pick her up and tell her—oh, such a host of things! But he was a wise House Surgeon, and his experience on the stairs had not counted for nothing; moreover, he was a great believer in the psychological moment, so he peered over her shoulder and tried to make out what she was looking at.

"Faded flowers," he volunteered at last, somewhat doubtfully.

"A primrose ring," she contradicted. "But who ever heard of one in a hospital? Take care—" For the surgeon's shoe was carelessly knocking some of the blossoms out of place. "Don't you know that no one must disturb a primrose ring? It's sacred to Fancy; and there is no telling what is happening inside there to-night."

"What?" The House Surgeon asked it as breathlessly as any little boy might have. Science had goaded him hard along the road of established facts, thereby causing him to miss many pleasant things which he still looked back upon regretfully, and found himself eager for, at times. Of course, he had scoffed at them aloud and before Margaret MacLean, but inwardly he adored them.

She did not answer; she was too busy wondering about something to hear the House Surgeon's question. Her eyes looked very big and round in the darkness, and her face wore the little-girl scarey look as she reached up for his hand and clutched it tight, while her other hand pointed across the primrose ring to the row of beds.

"See, they look empty, quite——quite empty."

"Just nerves." And he patted the hand in his reassuringly; he tried his best to pat it in the old, big-brother way. "You've had an awfully trying day—most women would be in their rooms having hysteria or doldrums."

Still she did not hear. Her eyes were traveling from cot to crib and on to cot again, as they had once before that night. "Every single bed looks empty," she repeated. "The clothes tumbled as if the children had slipped quietly out from under them." She shivered ever so slightly. "Perhaps they have found out they are not wanted any longer and have run away."

"Come, come," the House Surgeon spoke in a gruff whisper. "I believe you're getting feverish." And mechanically his fingers closed over her pulse. Then he pulled her to her feet. "Go over to those beds this minute and see for yourself that every child is there, safe and sound asleep."

But she held back, laughing nervously. "No, no; we mustn't spoil the magic of the ring." Her voice trailed off into a dreamy, wistful monotone. "Who knows—Cinderella's godmother came to her when it was only a matter of ragged clothes and a party; the need here was far greater. Who knows?" She caught her breath with a sudden in-drawn cry. "Why, to-night is May Eve!"

"Why, of course it is!" agreed the House Surgeon, as if he had known it from the beginning.

"And who knows but the faeries may have come and stolen them all away?"

Now the House Surgeon was old in understanding, although he was young in years; and he knew it was wiser sometimes to give in to the whims of a tired, overwrought brain. He knew without being told—for Margaret MacLean would never have told—how tired and hopelessly heart-sick and mind-sick she was to-night. What he did not know, however, was how pitifully lonely and starved her life had always been; and that this was the hour for the full conscious reckoning of it.

She had often said, whimsically, "Those who are born with wooden instead of golden spoons in their mouths had better learn very young to keep them well scoured, or they'll find them getting so rough and splintered that they can't possibly eat with them." She had followed her own advice bravely, and kept happy; but now even the wooden spoon had been taken from her.

The House Surgeon lifted her up and put her gently into the rocker, while he sat down on the corner of the table, neighbor to the green Devonshire bowl.

Perhaps Margaret MacLean was not to find bitterness, after all; perhaps it would be his glad good fortune to keep it from her. It was surprising the way he felt his misery dwindling, and instantly he pulled up his courage—another hole.

"I think you said 'faeries,'" he suggested, seriously. "Why not faeries?"

She nodded in equal seriousness. "Why not? They always come May Eve to the lonely of heart; and even a hospital might have faeries once in a generation. Only—only why couldn't they have taken me with the children? It wasn't exactly fair to leave me behind, was it?"

Her lips managed to keep reasonably steady, but she was wishing all the time that the House Surgeon would go and leave her free to be foolishly childish and weak. She wanted to drop down beside Bridget's bed and sob out her trouble.

But the House Surgeon had a very permanent look as he went on soberly talking.

"Well, you see, they took the children first because they were all ready. Probably, very probably, they are sending for you later—special messenger. It's still some minutes before midnight; and that's the time things like that happen. Isn't it?"

"Perhaps." A little amused smile crept into the corners of her mouth while she rummaged about in some old memories for something she had almost forgotten. "Perhaps"—she began again—"they will send the Love-Talker."

"The what?"

"The Love-Talker. Old Cassie used to tell us about him, when I was an 'incurable.' He's a faery youth who comes on May Eve in the guise of some well-appearing young man and beguiles a maid back with him into faeryland. He's a very ardent wooer—so Cassie said—and there's no maid living who can resist him."

"Wish I'd had a course with him," muttered the House Surgeon under his breath. Then he gripped the table hard with both hands while the spirit of mischief leaped, flagrant, into his eyes. "Would you go with him—if he came?" he asked, intensely.

"If he came—if he came—" she repeated, dreamily. "How do I know what I would do? It would all depend upon the way he wooed."

Unexpectedly the House Surgeon jumped to his feet, making a considerable clatter.

"Hush! you'll waken the children."

"But they're not here," he reminded her.

"Yes, I know; but you might waken them, just the same."

Instead of answering, the House Surgeon stepped behind the rocker and lifted her out of it bodily; then his hands closed over hers and he lifted them to her eyes, thereby blind-folding them. "Now," he commanded, "take two steps forward."

She did it obediently; and then stood waiting for further orders.

"You are now inside this magical primrose ring; and you said yourself, a moment ago, there was no telling what might happen inside. Keep very still; don't move, don't speak. Remember you mustn't uncover your eyes, or the spell will be broken. Hark! Can you hear something—some one coming nearer and nearer and nearer?"

For the space of a dozen breaths nothing could be heard in Ward C; that is—unless one was tactless enough to mention the sound of two throbbing hearts. One fluttered, frightened and hesitating; the other thumped, steady and determined. Then out of the darkness came the striking of the hospital clock on the tower—twelve long, mournful tolls—and one of the House Surgeon's arms slipped gently about the shoulders of Margaret MacLean.

"Dearest, the Love-Talker has turned so completely human that he has to say at the outset he's not half good enough for you, But he wants you—he wants you, just the same, to carry back with him to his faery-land. It will be rather a funny little old faery-land, made up of work and poverty—and love; but, you see, the last is so big and strong it can shoulder the other two and never know it's carrying a thing. If you'll only come, dearest, you can make it the finest, most magical faeryland a man ever set up home-making in."

Another silence settled over Ward C.

"Well—" said the House Surgeon, breaking it at last and sounding a trifle nervous. "Well—"

"I thought you said I wasn't to move or speak, or the spell would be broken?"

"That's right, excellent nurse—followed doctor's orders exactly." He was smiling radiantly now, only no one could see. Slowly he drew her hands away from her eyes and kissed the lids. "You can open them if you solemnly promise not to be disappointed when you see the Love-Talker has stepped into an ordinary house surgeon's uniform and looks like the—devil." With a laugh the House Surgeon gathered her close in his arms.

"The devil was only a rebelling angel," she murmured, contentedly.

"But I'm not rebelling. Bless those trustees! If they hadn't put us both out of the hospital we might be jogging along for the next ten years on the wholesome, easily digested diet of friendship, and never dreamed of the feast we were missing—like this—and this—and—"

Margaret MacLean buried her face in the uniform with a sob.

"What is it, dearest? Don't you like them?"

"I—love—them. Don't you understand? I never belonged to anybody before in all my life, so no one ever wanted to—"

The rest was unintelligible, but perfectly satisfactory to the House Surgeon. He held her even closer while she sobbed out the tears that had been intended for the edge of Bridget's bed; and when they were spent he wiped away all traces with some antiseptic gauze that happened to be in his pocket.

"I will never be foolish again and remember what lies behind to-night," said Margaret MacLean, knowing full well that she would be, and that often, because of the joy that would lie in remembering and comparing. "Now tell me, did they make you go, too?"

"The President told me, very courteously, that he felt sure I would be wishing to find another position elsewhere better suited to my rising abilities; and if an opportunity should come—next month, perhaps—they would not wish in any way to interfere with my leaving."

"Ugh! I—"

"No, you don't, dearest. You couldn't expect them to want us around after the things we magnanimously refrained from saying—but so perfectly implied."

"All right, I'll love them instead, if you want me to, only—" And she puckered her forehead into deep furrows of perplexity. "I have kept it out of my mind all through the evening, but we might as well face it now as to-morrow morning. What is going to happen to us?"

The House Surgeon turned her about until she was again looking across the line of scattered blossoms—into the indistinguishable darkness beyond. He laughed joyously, as a man can laugh when everything lies before him and there are no regrets left behind. "Have you forgotten so soon? We are to cross the primrose ring—right here; and follow the road—there—into faeryland after the children."

"The beds really do look empty."

"They certainly do."

"And we'll find the children there?"

"Of course."

"And I'll not have to give them up?"

"Of course not."

"And we'll all be happy together—somewhere?"

"Yes, somewhere!"

She turned quickly and reached out her arms to him hungrily. "I know now why a maid always follows the Love-Talker when he comes a-wooing."

"Why, dearest?"

"Because he makes her believe in him and the country where he is taking her, and that's all a woman asks."

X
WHAT HAPPENED AFTERWARD

Everybody woke with a start on the morning following the 30th of April; things began to happen even before the postman had made his first rounds. The operators at the telephone switchboards were rushed at an unconscionably early hour, considering that their station compassed the Avenue. The President was trying to get the trustees, Saint Margaret's, and the Senior Surgeon; the trustees were trying to get one another; while the Senior Surgeon was rapidly covering the distance between his home and the hospital—his mind busy with a multitude of things, none of which he had ever written with capitals.

Saint Margaret's was astir before its usual hour; there was a tang of joyousness in the air, and everybody's heart and mind, strangely enough, seemed to be in festal attire, although nobody was outwardly conscious of it. It was all the more inexplicable because Saint Margaret's had gone to bed miserable, and events naturally pointed toward depression: Margaret MacLean's coming departure, the abandoning of Ward C, the House Surgeon's resignation, and Michael's empty crib.

Ward C had wakened with a laugh. Margaret MacLean, who had been moving noiselessly about the room for some time, picking up the withered remains of the primrose ring, looked up with apprehension. The tears she had shed over Michael's crib were quite dry, and she had a brave little speech on the end of her tongue ready for the children's awakening. Eight pairs of sleepy eyes were rubbed open, and then unhesitatingly turned in the direction of the empty crib in the corner.

"Michael has gone away." she said, softly, steadying her voice with great care. "He has gone where he will be well—and his heart sound and strong."

She was wholly unprepared for the children's response. It was so unexpected, in fact, that for the moment she tottered perilously near the verge of hysterics. The children actually grinned; while Bridget remarked, with a chuckle:

"Ye are afther meanin' that he didn't come back—that's what!" And then she added, as an afterthought, "He said to tell ye 'God bless ye,' Miss Peggie."

Margaret MacLean did not know whether to be shocked or glad that the passing of a comrade had brought no sign of grief. Instead of being either, she went on picking up the primroses and wondering. As for the children, they lay back peacefully in their beds, their eyes laughing riotously. And every once in a while they would look over at one another, giving the funniest little expressive nods, which seemed to say: "I know what you're thinking about, and you know what I'm thinking about, so what's the need of talking. But when is it going to happen?"

The House Surgeon brought up her mail; it was an excuse to see her again before his official visit. "Are the children very much broken up over it?" he asked, anxiously, outside the door.

For answer Margaret MacLean beckoned him and pointed to the eight occupied cots—unquestionably serene and happy.

"Well, I'll be—" began the House Surgeon, retiring precipitously back to the door again; but the nurse put a silencing finger over his lips.

"Hush, dear! The children are probably clearer visioned than we are. I have the distinct feeling this morning of being very blind and stupid, while they seem—oh, so wise."

The House Surgeon grunted expressively. "Well, perhaps they won't take your going away so dreadfully to heart—now; or theirs, for that matter."

"I hope not," and then she smiled wistfully. "But I thought you told me last night we were all going together? At any rate, I am not going to tell them anything. If it must be it must be, and I shall slip off quietly, when the children are napping, and leave the trustees to tell."

She looked her mail over casually; there were the usual number of advertisements, a letter from one of the nurses who had gone South, and another in an unfamiliar hand-writing. She tore off the corner of the last, and, running her finger down the flap, she commented:

"Looks like quality. A letter outside the profession is a very rare thing for me."

She read the letter through without a sound, and then she read it again, the House Surgeon watching, the old big-brother look gone for ever from his face, and in its place a worshipful proprietorship. The effect of the letter was undeniably Aprilish; she looked up at the House Surgeon with the most radiant of smiles, while her eyes spilled recklessly over.

"How did you know it? How did you know it?" she repeated.

He was trying his best to find out what it was all about when one of the nurses came hurrying down the corridor.

"You are both wanted down in the board-room. They have called a special meeting of the trustees for nine o'clock; everybody's here and acting decidedly peculiar, I think. Why, as I passed the door I am sure I saw the President slapping the Senior Surgeon on the back. I never heard of anything like this happening before."

"Come," said Margaret MacLean to the House Surgeon. "If we walk down very slowly we will have time enough to read the letter on the way."

As the nurse had intimated, it was an altogether unprecedented meeting. Formality had been gently tossed out of the window; after which the President sat, not behind his desk, but upon it—an open letter in his hand. His whole attitude suggested a wish to banish, as far as it lay within his power, the atmosphere of the previous afternoon.

"Here is a letter to be considered first," he said, a bit gravely. "It makes rather a good prologue to our reconsideration of the incurable ward," and the ghost of a smile twitched at the corners of his mouth. "This is from the widow of the Richest Trustee." He read, slowly:

"MESDAMES AND GENTLEMEN OF THE BOARD,—I thank you for your courtesy in asking me to fill my husband's place as one of the trustees of Saint Margaret's. Until this afternoon I had every intention of so doing; but I cannot think now that my husband would wish me to continue his support of an institution whose directors have so far forgotten the name under which they dispense their charity as to put science and pride first. As for myself—I find I am strongly interested in incurables—your incurables. Yours very truly"

The President laid the letter behind him on the desk, while the entire board gasped in amazement.

"Well, I'll be hanged!" muttered the Disagreeable Trustee.

"But just think of *her*—writing it!" burst forth the Oldest Trustee.

The Meanest Trustee barked out an exclamation, but nothing followed it; undoubtedly that was due to the President's interrupting:

"I think if we had received this yesterday we should have been very—exceedingly—indignant; we should have censured the writer severely. As it is—hmm—" The President stopped short; it was as if his mind had refused to tabulate his feelings.

"As it is"—the Executive Trustee took up the dropped thread and went on—"we have decided to reconsider the removal of the incurable ward without any—preaching—or priming of conscience."

"I am so glad we really had changed our minds first. I should so hate to have that insignificant little woman think that we were influenced by anything she might write. Wouldn't you?" And the Youngest and Prettiest Trustee dimpled ravishingly at the Senior Surgeon.

"Wouldn't you two like to go into the consulting-room and talk it over? We could settle the business in hand, this time, without your assistance, I think." The voice of the Disagreeable Trustee dripped sarcasm.

"I should suggest," said the President, returning to the business of the meeting, "that the ward might be continued for the present, until we investigate the home condition of the patients and understand perhaps a little more thoroughly just what they need, and where they can be made most—comfortable."

"And retain Margaret MacLean in charge?" The Meanest Trustee gave it the form of a question, but his manner implied the statement of a disagreeable fact.

"Why not? Is there any one more competent to take charge?" The Executive Trustee interrogated each individual member of the board with a quizzical eye.

"But the new surgical ward—and science?" The Youngest and Prettiest threw it, Jason-fashion, and waited expectantly for a clash of steel.

Instead the Senior Surgeon stepped forward, rather pink and embarrassed. "I should like to withdraw my request for a new surgical ward. It can wait—for the present, at least."

And then it was that Margaret MacLean and the House Surgeon entered the board-room.

The President nodded to them pleasantly, and motioned to the chairs near him. "We are having what you professional people call a reaction. I hardly know what started it; but—hmmm—" For the second time that morning he came to a dead stop.

Everybody took great pains to avoid looking at everybody else; while each face wore a painful expression of sham innocence. It was as if so many naughty children had been suddenly caught on the wrong side of the fence, the stolen fruit in their pockets. It was gone in less time than it takes for the telling; but it would have left the careful observer, had he been there, with the firm conviction that, for the first time in their conservative lives, the trustees of Saint Margaret's had come perilously near to giving themselves away.

In a twinkling the board sat at ease once more, and the President's habitual composure returned. "Will some one motion that we adopt the two measures we have suggested? This is not parliamentary, but we are all in a hurry."

"I motion that we keep the incurables for the present, and that Miss MacLean be requested to continue in charge." There was a note of relieved repression in the voice of the Executive Trustee as he made the motion; and he stretched his shoulders unconsciously.

"But you mustn't make any such motion." Margaret MacLean rose, reaching forth protesting hands. "You would spoil the very best thing that has happened for years and years. Just wait—wait until you have heard."

As she unfolded her letter the President's alert eye promptly compared it with the one behind him on the desk. "So—you have likewise heard from the widow of the Richest Trustee?"

She looked at him, puzzled. "Oh, you know! She has written you?"

"Not what she has written you, I judge. One could hardly term our communication 'the best thing that has happened in years.'" And again a smile twitched at the corners of the President's mouth.

"Then listen to this." Margaret MacLean read the letter eagerly:

"DEAE MARGARET MACLEAN,—There is a home standing on a hilltop—an hour's ride from the city. It belongs to a lonely old woman who finds that it is too large and too lonely for her to live in, and too full of haunting memories to be left empty. Therefore she wants to fill it with incurable children, and she would like to begin with the discarded ward of Saint Margaret's."

"That's a miserable way to speak of a lot of children," muttered the Disagreeable Trustee; but no one paid any attention, and Margaret MacLean went on:

"There is room now for about twenty beds; and annexes can easily be added as fast as the need grows. This lonely old woman would consider it a great kindness if you will take charge; she would also like to have you persuade the House Surgeon that it is high time for him to become Senior Surgeon, and the new home is the place for him to begin. Together we should be able to equip it without delay; so that the children could be moved direct from Saint Margaret's. It is the whim of this old woman to call it a 'Home for Curables'—which, of course, is only a whim. Will you come to see me as soon as you can and let us talk it over?"

Margaret MacLean folded the letter slowly and put it back in its envelope. "You see," she said, the little-girl look spreading over her face—"you see, you mustn't take us back again. I could not possibly refuse, even if I wanted to; it is just what the children have longed for—and wished for—and—"

"We are not going to give up the ward; she would have to start her home with other children." The Dominant Trustee announced it flatly.

Strangely enough, the faces of his fellow-directors corroborated his assertion. Often the value of a collection drops so persistently in the estimate of its possessor that he begins to contemplate exchanging it for something more up to date or interesting. But let a rival collector march forth with igniting enthusiasm and proclaim a desire for the scorned objects, and that very moment does the possessor tighten his grip on them and add a decimal or two to their value. So was it with the trustees of Saint Margaret's. For the first time in their lives they desired the incurable ward and wished to retain it.

"Not only do we intend to keep the children, but there are many improvements I shall suggest to the board when there is more time. I should like to insist on a more careful supervision of—curious visitors." And the Oldest Trustee raised her lorgnette and compassed the gathering with a look that challenged dispute.

Margaret MacLean's face became unaccountably old and tired. The vision that had seemed so close, so tangible, so ready to be made actual, had suddenly retreated beyond her reach, and she was left as empty of heart and hand as she had been before. For a moment her whole figure seemed to crumple; and then she shook herself together into a resisting, fighting force again.

"You can't keep the children, after this. Think, think what it means to them—a home in the country, on a hilltop, trees and birds and flowers all about. Many of them could wheel themselves out of doors, and the others could have hammocks and cots under the trees. Forget for this once that you are trustees, and think what it means to the children."

"But can't you understand?" urged the President, "we feel a special interest in these children. They are beginning to belong to us—as you do, yourself, for that matter."

The little-girl look came rushing into Margaret MacLean's face, flooding it with wistfulness. "It's a little hard to believe—this belonging to anybody. Yesterday I seemed to be the only person who wanted me at all, and I wasn't dreadfully keen about it myself." Then she clapped her hands with the suddenness of an idea. "After all, it's the children who are really most concerned. Why shouldn't we ask them? Of course I know it is very much out of the accustomed order of things, but why not try it? Couldn't we?"

Anxiously she scanned the faces about her. There was surprise, amusement, but no dissent. The Disagreeable Trustee smiled secretly behind his hand; it appealed to his latent sense of humor.

"It would be rather a Balaam and his ass affair, but, as Miss MacLean suggests, why not try it?" he asked.

Margaret MacLean did not wait an instant longer. She turned to the House Surgeon. "Bring Bridget down, quickly."

As he disappeared obediently through the door she faced the trustees, as she had faced them once before, on the day previous. "Bridget will know better than any one else what will make the children happiest. Now wouldn't it be fun"—and she smiled adorably—"if you should all play you were faery godparents, for once in your lifetime, and give Bridget her choice, whatever it may be?"

This time the entire board smiled back at her; somehow, in some strange way, it had caught a breath of Fancy. And then—the House Surgeon re-entered with Bridget in his arms, looking very scared until she spied "Miss Peggie."

The President did the nicest thing, proving himself the good man he really was. He crossed hands with the House Surgeon, thereby making a swinging chair for Bridget, and together they held her while Margaret MacLean explained:

"It's this way, dear. Some one has offered you—and all the children—a home in the country—a home of your very own. But the trustees of Saint Margaret's hardly want to give you up; they think they can take as good care of you—and make you just as happy here."

"But—sure—they'll have to be givin' us up. Weren't we afther givin' a penny to the wee one yondther for the home?" and Bridget pointed a commanding finger toward the door.

Everybody looked. There on the threshold stood the widow of the Richest Trustee.

"What do you mean, dear? How could you have given her a penny?" Margaret MacLean asked it in bewilderment.

"'Twas all the doin's o' the primrose ring." And then Bridget shouted gaily across to the gray wisp of a woman. "Ye tell them. Weren't ye afther givin' us the promise of a home?"

"And haven't I come to keep the promise?" she answered, as gaily. But in an instant she sobered as her eyes fell on the open letter on the President's desk. "I am so sorry I wrote it—that is why I have come; not that I don't think you deserved it, for you do," and the widow of the Richest Trustee looked at them unwaveringly.

If she was conscious of the surprised faces about, she gave no sign for others to reckon by. Instead, she walked the length of the board-room to the President's desk and went on speaking hurriedly, as if she feared to be interrupted before she had said all she had come to say. "I wish I had written in another way, a more helpful way. Why not add your second surgical ward to Saint Margaret's and do all the good work you can, as you had planned? Only let me have these children to start a home which shall be a future harbor for all the cases you cannot mend with your science and which you ought not to set adrift. You can send me all the convalescing children, too, who need country air and building up. In return for this, and because you deserve to be punished—just a little—for yesterday—I shall try my best to take with me Margaret MacLean and your House Surgeon."

She laid a hand on both, while she added, softly: "Suppose we three go home together and talk things over. Shall we?"

So the "Home for Curables" has come true. It crests a hilltop, and is well worth the penny that Bridget gave for it. As the children specified, there are no "trusters"; and it has all the modern improvements, including Margaret MacLean, who is still "Miss Peggie," although she is married to their new Senior Surgeon.

There is one very particular thing about the Home which ought to be mentioned. When the children arrived Toby was on the steps, barking a welcome. No one was surprised; in fact, everybody acted as though he belonged there. Perhaps the surprising thing would have been not having the promise kept. Toby is allowed right of way, everywhere; and rumor has it that he often sneaks in at night and sleeps on Peter's bed. But, of course, that is just rumor.

The children are supremely happy; which means that no one is allowed to cross the threshold who cannot give the password of a friend. And you might like to know that many of the trustees of Saint Margaret's come as often as anybody, and are always welcomed with a shout. The President, in particular, has developed the habit of secreting things in his pockets until he comes looking very bulgy.

Margaret MacLean always puts the children to sleep with Sandy's song; she said it was written by a famous poet who loved children, and the children have never told her the truth about it. And if it happens, as it does once in a great while, that some one is missing in the morning, there is no sorrowing for him, or heavy-heartedness. They miss him, of course; but they picture him running, sturdy-limbed, up the slope to the leprechaun's tree, with Michael waiting for him not far off.

To the children Tir-na-n'Og is the waiting-place for all child-souls until Saint Anthony is ready to gather them up and carry them away with him to the "Blessed Mother"; and Margaret MacLean, having nothing better to tell them, keeps silent. But she has thought of the nicest custom: A new picture is hung in the Home after a child has gone. It bears his name; and it is always something that he liked—birds or flowers or ships or some one from a story. Peter has his chosen already; it is to be—a dog.

Whenever Saint Margaret's Senior Surgeon finds a hip or a heart or a back that he can do nothing for, he sends it to the Home; and he always writes the same thing:

"Here is another case in a thousand for you, Margaret MacLean. How many are there now?"

He has married the Youngest and Prettiest Trustee, as the Disagreeable Trustee prophesied, and gossip says that they are very happy. This much I know—there are two more words which he now writes with capitals—Son and Sympathy.

Margaret MacLean often says with the Danish faery-man: "My life, too, is a faery-tale written by God's finger." And the House Surgeon always chuckles at this, and adds:

"Praise Heaven! He wrote me into it."

As for the widow of the Richest Trustee, she has found a greater measure of contentment than she thought the world could hold—with love to brim it; for Margaret MacLean has adopted her along with the children. The children still regard her, however, as a very mysterious person; and she has taken the place of Susan's mythical aunt in the ward conversation. It has never been argued out to the complete satisfaction of every one whether she is really the faery queen or just the "Wee Gray Woman," as Sandy calls her. The arguments wax hot at times, and it is Bridget who generally has to put in the final silencing word:

"Faith, she kept her promise, didn't she? and everything come thrue, hasn't it? Well, what more do ye want?"